Missouri Folklore

Society Journal

Special Issue:

My Corner of the Porch

by

Loretta Washington

Volume 32

2010

Missouri Folklore Society Journal

Volume 32
2010

Special Issue:

My Corner of the Porch

by

Loretta Washington

Sketches by Don Carlson
Preface by Adam Brooke Davis

General Editors
Dr. Jim Vandergriff (Ret.)
Dr. Donna Jurich
University of Arizona

Missouri Folklore Society
P. O. Box 1757
Columbia, MO 65205

This issue of the *Missouri Folklore Society Journal* was published by Naciketas Press, 715 E. McPherson, Kirksville, Missouri, 63501

ISSN: 0731-2946; ISBN: 978-1-936135-25-7 (1-936135-25-6)

Library of Congress Control Number: 2016916281

The *Missouri Folklore Society Journal* is indexed in:

The *Hathi Trust Digital Library*: Vols. 4-24, 26; 1982-2002, 2004. This library essentially acts as an online keyword indexing tool; only allows users to search by keyword and only within one year of the journal at a time. The result is a list of page numbers where the search words appear. No abstracts or full-text incl. (Available free at http://catalog.hathitrust.org/Search/Advanced).

The *MLA International Bibliography*: Vols. 1-26, 1979-2004. Searchable by keyword, author, and journal title. The result is a list of article citations; it does not include abstracts or full-text.

RILM Abstracts of Music Literature: Vols. 13-14, 20; 1991-92, 1998. Searchable by keyword, author, and journal title. Indexes only selected articles about music that appear in these volumes only. Most of the entries have an abstract. There is no full-text.

A list of major articles in every issue of the journal also appears on the Society's web page. Go to *http://missourifolkloresociety.truman.edu/MFSJcnts.html.*

Notice to library subscribers and catalogers:
Though the cover date on this volume is 2010, the volume was actually published in 2016.

The Society's board is working to produce enough issues to catch up with the journal's publishing schedule as quickly as possible.

The Missouri Folklore Society is not responsible for the accuracy of statements of fact made by authors or book reviewers. Also, the opinions expressed in the Journal are those of the authors and do not necessarily reflect the opinions of the Society or its officers or members.

Dedication

To my small, but mighty family.

My Daughters, Laural and Lesley
My Grandchildren, Brienne, Joseph (Joey), Stephanie, Aaron, and
Corey
My Great Grandchildren, Travione (Tre), Amar, Cymphonii,
Brayden, Ashlyn, and Alanna

My Corner of the Porch

Contents

Thank You

I would like to take this opportunity to thank everyone who has helped me on this part of my life's journey.

Thank you, Adam Davis, Elizabeth Delmonico and Don Carlson. I have worked the closest with the three of you. Thank you, for your patience and understanding. We burned a lot of midnight oil via, the internet, phone, text, and snail mail, but it was not in vain. We did it. I feel fortunate to have had the opportunity to get to know and work with each of you. I learned a great deal.

Collectively, I have learned volumes from you. I will always be thankful and appreciative for having had the opportunity to learn from such a learned group of educators. I am eternally grateful for this once in a lifetime experience. The diverse amount of helpful information will definitely be of service to me in the future. I proudly move forward with a greater understanding of life, writing, storytelling, and the publishing processes. In the future I will use the knowledge I have gained wisely.

Individually, I thank each of you for exposing me to different learning opportunities. Each aspect taught me to have a greater appreciation of all knowledge gained. With an open mind, one cannot limit or put a price tag on knowledge. Knowledge is endless and it's priceless. Knowing this has taught me not to squander what I gain and to cherish every morsel of it. I thank each of you for helping me to see that writing my stories was the easy part. Going through the processes to get what I had written published was the real lesson. This knowledge can't be measured. As I move forward, I would like to thank each of you for awaking in me, a greater appreciation and understanding of everything involved, in getting a book to the press.

To my friends and everyone else who have helped me on my journey?

You all remind me of the saying, "it takes a village to raise a child." Whenever I needed anything, you all were always there. Without you I would not have been able to reach this part of my journey. Being a part of the village, know that I will always be here for you.

I send a very special thank you to Becky Schroeder. Becky, you planted a seed within me for this book in 2010. Through the years you nourished that seed as much as you were able to. I want you to know that the seed did grow. Thank you.

To my family, I cannot say thank you enough; each of you play a very important role in my life. Know that I'm grateful and appreciate all of you. It's a blessing to know that all of you are always there for me. Family, we have come this far by grace and faith. I know we will hold on together and see what the end is going to be.

I thank everyone who has helped me in any way. Your contributions to my book were needed and appreciated. Be it great or small, without your help, *My Corner of the Porch* would not be in print today.

Warmest Regards To All.
Loretta Washington – 2016

Preface

Storytellers live interesting lives. Which is to say, things happen to all of us, but interesting things happen to people who can *tell*. It's not that interesting events make ordinary people into storytellers. It's that storytellers make ordinary events interesting.

How?

I do not know how the rather strange book *Oh Sir, You've Shot Her!* came my way when I was eight or nine. It's the reminiscences of a small boy in a slightly dotty upper-middle class family in Copenhagen, about 1890. The events are both outrageous and perfectly credible. There is a leg-biting, preverbal little-brother, a father who plays with firearms in the house, and a malicious old grandmother who is going to end up getting killed by the end of the story, and by the narrator. (Have we got you looking it up on Ebay yet?) The writer, Benjamin Jacobsen, would go on to become famous for other things, things which never appear, even by hints, in the narration. He manages to re-enter the mind of a small boy to whom the everyday is wondrous and the wondrous unremarkable, and for whom the respected scholar he is destined to become does not exist and would not be very interesting if he did.

Another favorite was the Follett Award winner, *Me and Caleb*. My 4th grade teacher read this aloud to a bunch of kids who thought themselves much too old to be read to. But however stubbornly we might resist the enchantment, we were spellbound by young Bud Wallings. He had a *speaking* voice, and more than one critic has called him a distant relative of Tom and Huck. These were yarns of a depression-era Ozarks boyhood, a little grittier, a little more recognizable than Twain's idylls (though those were not entirely alien even to a suburban St. Louis boy in the 60s, especially one who spent summers with grandparents in Hannibal). It's a less genteel world than haute-bourgeois Denmark. But Bud and his brother Caleb are as unaware that they're poor as little Benjamin Jacobsen grasps that he's privileged. A child's horizons are closer than that, and therefore the world's seen in tighter detail. It's a forest of legs; your great aunt and the piano look much the same from that angle. These tales unrolled in the same atmosphere my father conjured at the dinner table, telling of long-gone days (only a quarter century behind at that time, now lost in the mists of eight decades). Franklyn Meyer was writing of places very like Montauk and Turtle, where my great-grandfather held brief and some-times tumultuous pastorates (recalled very differently by the old-timers I interviewed, who had something very much other than a child's perspec-tive on those days and events). Meyer, like Jacobsen, had the storyteller's gift of teleporting the reader, yes.

But you know what? That's overrated. It's descriptive skill, no mean thing, but still mere technique. It's like juggling; given enough practice, dogged time-on-task, anybody can learn to do it well enough to impress the uninitiated. What lifts these relatively unknown memoirs I've been talking about, and also distinguishes the brand-new-old stories you're now holding in your hand — oh fortunate reader, you who still have the happy pleasure ahead of you — is that true magic I mentioned before: the writer's capacity to re-occupy the lost child-self.

Is that to say storytellers are born, not made? I think it's both. There's a gift, but it has to be cultivated, in the right environment, in the right apprenticeship. Such was Loretta's good fortune, to have her great grand-mother and her grandmother as childhood models, and in adulthood to be coached by Gladys Coggswell, under the auspices of the Missouri Arts Council's Traditional Arts Apprenticeship Program.

There are of course indelible characters, and a setting that's made vivid with very few strokes of the pen, like an impressionist drawing. Tiny Aint Tankie looms over all, naturally, like a near mountain, sheltering, threat-ening if and when she chooses to be, setting definite limits. There's a social world. Little Loretta outranks Doris Faye — ever-compliant, eager simply to be in the company of, in cahoots with, her older cousin. Brother Junior has a poignant place, evidently still open to the pleasures of childhood and imagination, the occasional adventure, but also increasingly aware of his adult dignity.

From the folklorist's point of view, these tales have documentary value. For instance, when rain falls while the sun shines brightly, what do you call that? In folklore we look for some combination of conservation and variation. Informants report "the devil's getting married," the "devil's beating his wife" and "the devil's beating his wife behind the door" as habitual comments on such occasions. A chapter here gives an answer with a location in time and space, all the documentarian wants, but more: the context of wonder, of possibility, a tinge of fear tempered by the knowledge that someone as powerful as Aint Tankie had authorized the expedition, and nothing untoward could therefore happen.

That story again takes us to the world of childhood where primal forces — the Devil, the Rain — could be encountered in your front yard. There are moral elementals, too. For my money, "Don't Go Under the House" taps into the wellsprings of narrative more effectively than any of these others. Once upon a time, there were a boy and a girl, innocent, and a powerful and beloved elder told them not to do something. Wasn't something they particularly wanted to do anyhow, and the elder was known to be wise and loving. But you know, something about people, you tell them no ... . There was a snake involved.

No, it's not a retelling of the Fall, except that each of us experiences disobedience and redemption as an absolutely necessary part of the process of ceasing to be a dependent and obedient child and becoming an adult whose compliance is as chosen and authentic as her rebellion. It exploits the same powerful images and mechanisms, gently, though, with a dual consciousness that assures us the consequences are not really going to be as dire as the narrator believes. It is what Greek narratology called the *katabasis*, the downward journey the seeker must make in order to confront death and destiny. And yet it's not literary, a conscious deployment of that device or a sly reference to a prior text that people in the know will ... well, know. It's a storyteller's instinctive recognition of the fundamental laws of storytelling that guided Homer, Vergil, and the author of the Pentateuch. Odysseus and Aeneas would have fully understood the capslock of DON'T GO UNDER THE HOUSE, and the ominous phrase known to all children everywhere, which is actually engraved in consciousness in 24-point type: the prospect of BIG TROUBLE. Now read the story of "Making Sweet Peach Juice" — another replay of Eden, forbidden fruit indeed.

For all the scampiness, domestic mischief, rulebending curiosity and mouthiness, there are other kinds of narrative here, less physical comedy, more an exploration of fundamental morality. Who could be unmoved by the child's refusal to exploit the opportunity to investigate a mysterious trunk — an act of pure piety? In another telling, the motif might be cautionary, as with Pandora, or might produce the sheer terror that drives the Bluebeard taletype. Stories of wrongdoing that is irreversible and yet forgivable, captured in a domestic event: the seasoned skillet ... ah, I broke my mother's. It was like breaking Excalibur, That Which Cannot Be Broken. She never said a word, but she grieved, and so do I, to this day.

In editing the volume, we sometimes had questions about the lifeworld Loretta put before us. There were a number of references to Aint Tankie's use of a snuffbrush. I asked Loretta to sketch one for me, so I could visualize it. She demurred: "I can't draw a straight line with a ruler." But when you ask a storyteller a question...

> But I think I can help you envision what a snuffbrush is. It's a small branch from a tree. When I was growing up in Wardell, weeping willow trees were pretty much everywhere. Most of the time my great grandmother and Aint Tankie used a small branch from a weeping willow tree for their snuffbrushes. [...] different woods like different brands have a different taste and texture. Some "green" woods have a stronger bitter taste than other green woods. I know this because like most kids I also tried my hand at what they called "dipping snuff." So, as a child I made a few snuffbrushes, some good, some not so good.
>
> The branches they used were smaller than a pencil, but thicker than the lead in a pencil. If you or anyone you know ever watched the TV program *Survivor*, you have seen this kind of wooden brush. It's what the survivors use every day to clean their teeth with, but of course without the snuff. I often saw my great grandmother and grandmother clean their teeth with their brush with snuff on it. I also tried that as a child. I don't know if this process helped, but both of them had most of their teeth when they passed at ages 91 & 93.

And also typically, when a storyteller tells a story, it leads to another story. In an emailed response to my inquiry, she continued: "Below is an excerpt from 'Ellen,' a story I wrote about my great grandmother telling me stories, and her death. It describes the snuffbrush and how it's used:"

> I remember this so well because sometimes before Mama would start a story, she would call me to her side and say, "I think this old snuffbrush is worn out. Baby, would you go get me a branch off that old weeping willow tree in the back?"
>
> I would run down the steps of that old wooden porch and around to the back of the house to the weeping willow tree. I would stand there nervously, looking up for a few seconds, trying to find just the right size branch. Mama had sent me on an important mission and I had to make sure I took her the right branch.
>
> When I thought I had spotted the perfect branch I would jump up, pull it down and break off a piece. Then I would run back to Mama and say, "Is this all right Mama? Is this all right?" Now, when I think back, she didn't care what size that branch was. Mama would always say "that's just fine baby, just fine."
>
> Mama would then sit down in her rocking chair, go into her apron pocket and take out her little pocket knife and cut off a 3-4 inch piece of the branch. Mama would peel off the green bark and then, she would start chewing one end of it. She would chew it until it was as fine as the bristles of a tooth-brush.
>
> Then she would reach back into her apron pocket for her old snuff-box. She would take it out and tap the top several times, then take the top off and lay it down. With one hand she would pull down her bottom lip and hold it and with her other hand she would put snuff in her lip from her snuff box. She packed the snuff in place with her tongue until it was just right.
>
> When this was done she would pick up her snuff brush and roll it around in the snuffbox and then place it in the corner

of her mouth. Once this was done, then the story could start. But, while this was taking place, I always sat quietly beside her on my little wooden stool. I watched and waited patiently and the wait was always worth the story that I heard.

As a storyteller might say, as Loretta might explain, I told you that so I can tell you this: the whole book is in Loretta's voice, depends on that voice. We want you to hear that voice — these are talking tales. Washington has a gift for what creative writing teachers call "build" and suspense, and she renders the bounded world of childhood in all its intensity. Her typography and punctuation replicate a dimension of what print can never really deliver, the storyteller's performance in full human presence. In fact, as we edited, we deleted, then restored a great many commas, as soon we realized they were marking oratorical patterns, breathing points for declamation. This was the voice, the very thing that made the work valuable, and must of course be respected. So please don't suppose we're still learning to copyedit over here.

We did learn much in the process of editing. I think it's fair to say there were some misunderstandings in the process of bringing the memories, the vision, the spoken voice to the printed page. That's what happens with good editing; like a friendship or even a marriage it's a melding of sometimes contradictory understandings. Like those things, there are going to be some rocks in the path. Best accept that. The wonder of all art is to take something that is inside one's own head and make it materialize in somebody else's. What greater magic can there be?

"Imagination" means to make images appear. At our request, retired art teacher, social worker, and editor—Don Carlson did that here. At the edge of a ninth decade, he has torn off the same calendar pages as Loretta, and a few more. He remembers much of what she remembers—the wood stoves, outhouses, oil lamps and cast iron skillets, the need for discipline. Yet an author and an illustrator must always and inevitably play this game called "Izzisit? Izzisit?" As emails with attached scans and snail mails with sketches flew back and forth, Don became steadily more committed to creating the texture of Loretta's remembrance, as opposed to re-presenting his own. He found his idiom in figures with sharp or faded outlines. His illustrations have that quality of memory and dream where some things leap forward in stark detail, others retreat into fog, and no wise person presumes to explain which and why. His impressionistic renderings feel simultaneously improvised and authentic, serious and whimsical, permanent and changeable. They are the ink pen's version of the speaking voice.

So the pictures mirror the aesthetic of oral delivery, the feel of ex tempore composition. Like Loretta's stories, they do not feel memorized.

Thus, what happens on *My Corner of the Porch* comes through as spontaneous and as related to previous performances, but always as unique to the occasion, the audience, the moment. The tales are put down here as a speaker would address a listening audience, with repetition and rhythms that aren't part of the written — it's not a text, it's performance. Sustained, lyric, it's a loveletter to childhood and to family, and above all to querulous, capricious, wise, and loving Aint Tankie.

Adam Brooke Davis
Kirksville, September 2016

The Wrath of May Tankie Belle Walker

She was four feet, ten inches tall and in her own words she used to say, "I never weighed a hundred pounds, even when I was soaking wet." She was small in stature and behind her back we sometime referred to her as "that little woman." But whenever we upset that little woman, she roared like a lion and everyone listened. That was my grandmother.

As a child I spent six years in the Missouri Bootheel with my grand-mother and great grandmother. Everyone always called my grandmother "Aint Tankie;" I can't remember anyone ever calling her anything else. To this day we still refer to her as Aint Tankie. I think it's just one of those country things.

During my time in the Missouri Bootheel, I learned many lessons from Aint Tankie. But, there was one lesson that it took me a few years to learn. That lesson was whenever that little woman told you not to do something, you better not do it. The last thing in the world you wanted to hear her say was "go get me a switch from that weeping willow tree in the back yard." If she ever told you to get three switches and told you that they better not be small, you were in BIG trouble.

Fear can be a powerful thing. Without touching us Aint Tankie could put a fear in us like nobody I have ever known. Most of the times when I got a scolding, I would think, "I wish she would just go on and give me a switching." I just wanted to get it over with. That may sound a little crazy to most people. But, Aint Tankie's tongue lashings would hurt me more than any switching she had ever given me. Whenever she gave me one of her good tongue lashings, the kind that hurt to the core of your spirit, I stayed out of trouble for a long time.

The look on my grandmother's face and the tone of her voice were so believable. So every time she scolded us or threatened to give us a switching, we believed her. In our minds, we never knew what that little woman was going to do until she stopped talking. She didn't know it, but we never really needed all of the admonishments that we received. With that stern look on her face and the convincing tone of her voice, we gladly accepted her smallest words of warning.

Later in life, I realized that the majority of the time my grandmother's threats were ONE BIG BLUFF. As children, we got very few switchings. Today when I think back about some of the dangerous things we did as kids, we properly deserved a scolding and a switching.

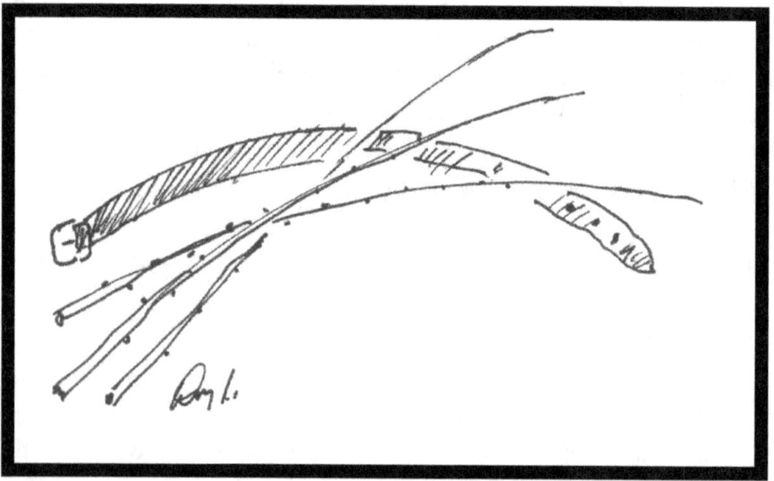

Remember, I said that if Aint Tankie told you not to do something, you better not do it. Well, most of the kids did as they were told, except for me. I had to be different. I always had to say something. I always had to challenge what my grandmother said. At the end of almost every statement she made, I did what most kids do today. I asked, "WHY?" I always questioned her, and sometimes, my questions were not related to what she had just said. I always pushed her just a little bit further and sometimes to her limit.

One of the days that I pushed my grandmother to her limit, started out like any other hot summer day. My brother Junior and I were playing in the back yard. Junior was doing whatever it is boys do when they play. But, me I was doing what I enjoyed the most and that was making mud pies. My grandmother was sitting on the front porch and she had told me several times to go in and wash the dishes. Well, I kept saying "Yes, Ma am," but I never stopped playing, so the dishes never got washed. It was starting to get close to that time of the day when Aint Tankie usually started cooking supper.

She called me one more time and said, "Loretta, didn't I tell you to go inside and wash them dishes?" I recognized the tone that she used and I knew that it was going to be the last time she was going to tell me to go wash the dishes. So I decided to stop making my mud pies and go do what I had been told to do several times.

But I was having fun, and I didn't want to stop making my mud pies and go inside to wash the dishes. So, when I started to get up, I developed a little attitude. I frowned and stuck out my bottom lip. I got up slowly and started walking toward the house. That's when my brother Junior started to laugh at me and then he started to tease me. As I walked passed him he started to sing, "You gotta do the dishes, you gotta do the dishes." Then, he laughed at me!

I looked at him and gave him a dirty look and said "you better leave me alone."

Then he said, "and if I don't, what you gonna do?"

Then he got up and walked over to my stack of beautiful mud pies and stepped on them and laughed again.

I had spent a lot of time making those mud pies. That day my mud mixture was perfect and I was going to come back later and play with them. I got so mad at him that I started to cry. Well, it just so happened that we had this wood pile in the back yard. When I walked past that wood pile, I reached over and picked up a piece of wood. I turned around and started walking back towards Junior.

By now, tears were running down my cheeks. I was yelling at him, "you better fix them, you better fix them."

My brother turned around and saw me coming towards him carrying that piece of wood. He started running towards the front of the house, yelling, "Aint Tankie, Aint Tankie, Loretta is trying to hit me with a BIG piece of wood."

By now I was running, and I had raised my arm up over my head with that piece of wood in my hand. I was crying and I was mad and I was after him.

When he turned the corner of the house I was right behind him. When I turned the corner of the house, I ran face first into my grandmother. Junior was behind her, hugging her. He peeped around her apron at me.

I gave him a dirty look and thought to myself, "I was so close. I was so close to him."

Aint Tankie grabbed my wrist and took the piece of wood out of my hand. That day, I got "the look." I calmed down enough to realize that this time I was in BIG TROUBLE. We had been told time and time again not to fight; all of us knew that fighting would get you into big trouble. My grandmother had always told us, "if somebody hit you, come and tell me and I'll take care of the problem." Not knowing exactly how she was going to "take care of the problem" kept us in line most of the time.

But, when I looked up into her eyes that day, it was one of the few times I was speechless. There was nothing I could say in my defense. I couldn't think of anything that would justify what I was trying to do to my brother. So, I just stood there crying, knowing that my tears were mostly from anger, because I didn't want to stop playing and go wash the dishes. Then to make matters worse, Junior had squished all of the mud pies and I couldn't get to him. I couldn't tell Aint Tankie that.

So I stood there looking into that little woman's eyes, and I could see that this time I was in really big trouble. In a firm voice, Aint Tankie said, "girl, what are you trying to do?" I looked up at her with tears streaming down my face and said, "Junior stepped on my mud pies." I thought I had her sympathy. I felt like that had given me the right to chase him with that piece of wood. But, deep down inside, I knew that what I was doing was wrong, but I still did it anyway.

Aint Tankie looked at me and then at the piece of wood; then she said, "What are you doing? You could have hurt your brother. Just think about how badly you could have hurt him if you had hit him in the head or face." Then she pointed to a sharp edge on the wood and said, "Look at this piece of wood, just look at it, look at it!" I stopped crying, but I was still sniffing. I looked at the sharp edge on the wood, then I looked at her and said, "Yes, ma'am."

Aint Tankie stopped scolding me and turned around and looked at Junior, and said, "Why did you step on her mud pies?"

Junior stared back at her and hunched his shoulders and said, "I don't know."

Shaking her finger in our faces she told both of us, "This is the reason why I tell you children, not to fight or hit each other. Come and tell me when something happens. I'm the one who decides what to do, not you all."

Aint Tankie looked at us and said in a loud voice, "didn't I tell you all that?" Junior and I both said, "Yes ma'am."

By now I was settling down a little and I was starting to think to myself, "I don't think she is going to send me to the corner of the porch today." I realized that what I had tried to do was wrong and dangerous. I didn't tell Aint Tankie, but I was ready to accept my punishment. So, I thought, "today I'm going to get a switching."

But instead, my grandmother looked at me and then at Junior, then she said, "Junior go get the belt."

I thought "what?"

That little woman had surprised me and caught me off guard. Aint Tankie usually sent you to get your own switch or the belt, when she was going to use it on you. So my little mind started ticking, trying to figure out, what she was going to do? It took me about a half minute, but I figured everything out. I was not going to get a switching after all. Junior had messed up my mud pies, so he was going to get three licks with the belt. He's going to get them, not me. So, I smiled inside.

At that point, I knew that I was going to get off with just being sent to the corner of the porch, again. To me, that made perfectly good sense. After all, she had sent him for the belt. Junior looked puzzled as he walked away. I could tell that he was wondering why she had sent him to get the belt. I knew that he was properly thinking, "She should have sent Loretta to get the belt, after all she was trying to hit me with that big piece of wood." That day my brother looked confused; he didn't know what was going to happen. But me, I smiled. I wasn't worried. I had everything all figured out. I thought to myself, "That's what he gets for stepping on my mud pies."

When Junior walked away, Aint Tankie just stood there looking at me.

She didn't say a word, but she didn't look like she was angry at me. I thought this would be a good time to make sure that Junior was going to get three licks and not me. So, I said, "Aint Tankie, why did you send Junior for the belt instead of me?" Aint Tankie looked at me and said, "Girl, don't ask me anything right now."

My grandmother's tone was firm, but it didn't sound like she was mad, so her answer didn't bother me. After all, I had already figured everything out. By then Junior returned with the belt in his hand. He started to hand it to Aint Tankie, but she told him to keep it. Then Aint Tankie turned and looked at me and said, "Junior, give Loretta three licks." Before I knew it I said, "What?"

When I heard what that little woman had just said, my eyes got as big as silver dollars and my legs got instantly weak. I couldn't believe my ears. She did something completely different that day. She had tricked me and I didn't see it coming.

Junior looked at Aint Tankie, and then he looked at me and said, "Uh, Uh."

Aint Tankie said it again, "give Loretta three licks."

As the tears started to form in my eyes I said, "Why can't I give him three licks?"

She swirled around and looked at me and said, "Didn't I tell you not to ask me anything?"

Then she turned back to my brother and said again in a louder voice, "Junior."

But, before she could finish her statement, I said, "then why can't you give me a spanking instead of Junior? Aint Tankie looked at me again, then she bent down close to my face and in a louder voice said, "Girl, this is the last time I'm gonna say this, don't ask me anything?"

I said, "Yes ma'am," then I started to cry.

I was scared. I couldn't believe what I was hearing, that little woman was going to let Junior give me a spanking. Junior was never, ever supposed to give me a spanking. I thought to myself, "This isn't right, it's not right!" The tears were rolling down my face like a river; I couldn't believe it. Junior was going to give me a spanking and I couldn't do anything about it.

My feelings were really hurt that day.

Aint Tankie said, "Junior, go on, give Loretta three licks."

Poor Junior didn't have a choice, so he gave me three licks. The licks really didn't hurt me. As a matter of fact Junior tapped me very lightly three times on top of all of my clothes. I barely felt his licks. But I wiggled. I screamed. I cried like he was killing me. My grandmother just stood there and she didn't stop him. Now, when I think back about that day, I didn't fool my grandmother, she knew that Junior wasn't hurting me. The whole time he was spanking me, I was thinking, how could she tell my brother to give me three licks with the belt? How could she let him do this to me? What was wrong with her? Why is she letting him give me three licks? It wasn't right, Junior was never supposed to do that. It wasn't right!

When he finished giving me my three licks I went on into the house, crying and rubbing my backside like it was really hurting. I couldn't feel any pain from the spanking, but that day my feelings were really hurting. I didn't stop crying until I was almost finished with the dishes. I still couldn't believe that my grandmother had let my brother give me three licks. It just wasn't right. When I finished washing the dishes I went and sat in my little rocking chair. I sat there and rocked, still sniffing in disbelief. I rocked and sniffed until I started to doze, then I got up and went back outside to remake my mud pies.

I never will forget that day. I stayed mad at my brother for a long time. I could see that he was hurting and had regrets, but he spanked me that day. I couldn't get over that, he was never supposed to spank me! Later I realized that something good did come from that day. I never picked up anything to hit or throw at my brother or cousin again. And my brother and cousin never hit each other again either. That is, none of us ever let Aint Tankie see or hear us, when we did. That little woman had pulled a switch on us that day. In our minds, we didn't know what she would do if we got caught hitting each other again.

Remember, I told you that I always asked "Why?" Well, the next summer around the same time we were putting wood on the wood pile. Those three licks crossed my mind. When Aint Tankie put her last piece of wood on the pile, I got up enough nerve to ask her why she let Junior spank me. Aint Tankie said, "What you almost did last year was dangerous; if you had hit your brother in the face or head with that piece of wood, you could have hurt him badly." You deserved a spanking and I wanted that spanking to be one that you would never forget." Then Aint Tankie said, "Besides that, I knew that if Junior spanked you, your feelings would be hurt. You needed to remember what you almost did."

Aint Tankie looked at me and her face looked different, it was soft. I didn't know it them, but what I saw was love. Then she said, "I know that you and your brother love each other. I also knew that he wouldn't hit you hard when he spanked you. But, the most important thing that day was that you needed to be taught a lesson more than anything else. It needed to be a lesson that you would never forget." She smiled and said, "I knew that if Junior spanked you, you would never forget that spanking and that's what I wanted." She looked at me and said, "Do you understand what I'm telling you? I answered, "Yes ma'am." Then she continued, "I wanted to make sure you remembered that day and that was the best thing I could come up with on such short notice."

All I can say is that it worked. I stayed out of trouble for a long time after that. I didn't want that to happen again, so I didn't take any chances. In my mind, I didn't want to do anything that would create another situation that would allow that little woman an opportunity to let my brother spank me again.

What almost happened that day was dangerous and I can truly say that I'm glad that my grandmother was there to stop me. And, I will never forget the day that my grandmother let my brother give me three licks with the belt.

As for always asking "why," to this today I still think "why" when I hear most things. But, after that day I've learned not to always ask "why" as much as I used to when I was a child.

My Corner of the Porch

I came back to live in St. Louis after the summer of my tenth birthday. But during my last two summers in the Missouri Bootheel, I spent a lot of time sitting on the corner of my grandmother's (Aint Tankie's) front porch. Aint Tankie started sending me to the corner of the porch, because I had this one little problem.

Now, I don't want anyone to misunderstand what I'm about to say, because I was really a good girl. I usually did what I was told to do. I rarely got into trouble. But, I did have this one little problem, I love to talk. I usually had something to say about everything. As a matter of fact, I always had something to say about everything. To be honest with you, I ran my mouth all the time, and most of the time, my talking got me into trouble.

The summer of my 8th birthday I spent a lot of time sitting on the corner of the porch. And there I was, on a hot summer afternoon, sitting on the corner of the porch, again. It seemed like lately I had been spending a lot of time there. I spent so much time sitting on the corner of the porch, that everyone started calling it "Loretta's corner of the porch."

My grandmother was always telling me, "Close your mouth. Stop talking so much. You need to watch what you say. I told you to shut-up. I'm not going to tell you to be quiet again. Didn't I tell you to stay in a child's place?" By the time I was ten years old, I was very familiar with all of these sayings and many more.

When I was seven years old I had no idea that Mama, my great grandmother, would be gone by my next birthday. But in January of 1953, Mama passed away. My great grandmother was my best friend and I thought she would always be there for me. I never thought about her dying or me missing her. So I was feeling a little lost without her. It didn't dawn on me how much Aint Tankie would miss her mother. But when it was time for the spring gardening, all of us could see that Aint Tankie missed her mother and was grieving.

Every spring Aint Tankie and Mama would plant a garden. Spring was here, but my great grandmother wasn't, so Aint Tankie asked me to help her. When I thought about me replacing my great grandmother in the garden and I got excited. I thought, now everyone will see that I'm a big girl. I'm big enough to take Mama's place in the garden. I was ready. I wanted to learn everything and help with everything. But I soon forgot about the one thing that I needed to learn to do first.

The day my mouth changed my young life started out like any other hot summer day. Aint Tankie and I had been working in the garden for most of the morning. It was getting close to noon and I was starting to get hot and tired. I thought to myself, "If I could stop working and go play for a while, I would cool off." But when I looked over at Aint Tankie, she was working as if it was the cool of the afternoon.

I was weeding and thinning out a row of greens when I started to fall behind. Aint Tankie looked over her shoulder and said, "Loretta, you need to pick up your speed, we have to weed the tomatoes and pepper plants today." I asked myself, "Why do we have to do them today?" I was hot. I was tired. I didn't feel like working in the garden anymore. What I really wanted to do was go play in the front yard with my cousin, Doris Faye. I looked up at Aint Tankie and thought, "all she wants to do is work, work, work."

When I think about what happened that day, all I can say is that I must have lost my mind for a few minutes from all of that heat. That day, it was hot in the garden. Just from watching Doris Faye play, I could see that it was cooler in the front yard. But it was so warm in the garden that the heat started to bother me and I started to sweat. I got so warm from that hot sun beaming down on the top of my head that I wasn't in my right mind.

I think I may have had a heat stroke or something that day. I do know that my right mind was gone for a minute. It had to be that, because if I had been in my right mind, I would have never listened to that little voice that said, "you know what you need to say, now go on, tell Aint Tankie." It was the heat that made me say what I said. Soon after I said it, I got this weird feeling, that it wasn't right. I'm telling you, it was that hot sun and the heat.

If I had been in my right mind, when my grandmother told me to "speed it up," I would have said "yes ma'am." But, instead! I stood up and put my little hands on my little hips. I turned around and looked right at my grandmother. In a loud, clear, voice I said, "This is YOUR garden, why do I have to work in it ALL day? I want to go PLAY with Doris Faye."

Oops! Immediately after I said it, I knew that I had made a BIG mistake. The tone and the words I used were "switching" words. I also knew that in a few minutes, if I could sit down, that I would be sitting on my corner of the porch, again. This time I knew that it wasn't going to be for a little while. With a little luck, I might get off the porch before dusk or before the mosquitoes ate me up.

I was wrong. I had overstepped my boundaries with my grandmother. Right after the words left my mouth, I was remorseful. But while I was thinking about being remorseful, Aint Tankie stood up and swirled around. She fixed her eyes on mine. I could see both hurt and anger on her face. Then in a loud, clear tone that was just a below a scream she said, "WHAT DID YOU SAY?" That's when I forgot about my heat stroke and started to shake. I knew that my troubles had just started.

Aint Tankie put one of her hands on her hip; the other hand was swinging at her side. Then, she started walking towards me. From her look, I knew what was in store for me. In order for Aint Tankie to reach me, she had to walk past an old weeping willow tree that sat in the middle of the garden. When my grandmother reached that old weeping willow, she reached over and broke off a branch. But she never looked at the tree. I stood there amazed. I thought to myself, how did she do that? During the whole time, her eyes stayed fixed on mine.

The year before, Mr. Fred had said that he was going to cut the tree down, but he never did. At that moment I thought, oh how I wished Mr. Fred had cut that old tree down last year. I shifted my eyes from hers for a second to look at the switch she was carrying. I could see that it was the right size and it had my name written all over it.

Deep down inside, I knew that this was one switching that I had earned all because I couldn't keep my mouth shut. I had to open my mouth and say what I wanted to say, but this time I went too far. I knew that I was wrong, but I still didn't want a switching. I knew that I had to do something, and in a hurry. If I didn't, this was going to be one switching that I wouldn't forget. So I decided to do what most kids do to this day when they get in trouble and think they may get punished for it. They start crying, falling out, screaming, jumping up and down and running all around the place. We didn't dare run back then, but we did all of the other things. I immediately started my drama by dancing and rubbing my legs as I prayed. This was followed by pleading, begging and more praying.

Then I added some tears as I pleaded saying, "please, please Aint Tankie. I don't want a switching. I promise I'll keep my mouth shut. I'm sorry. I promise you I won't talk so much. I promise I won't." While I was doing all of these things, I had not been touched; she was still walking towards me. By now she was closer and her face and eyes still said "switching." I could see that all of the drama was not working.

I thought to myself, it's time for more tears. So, I started to cry so hard that my throat hurt. And, the tears, oh the tears, came pouring out of my eyes, they were flowing like a running river. With all of that, she still didn't stop until she was right in front of me. I had to think fast; my time was up. I thought, the switching can start at any time now. At that very moment, I remembered the magical words. These words had saved me so many times in the past. They had gotten me out of trouble more times than I had deserved. But, most importantly they always melted my grandmother's heart. Many times they had stopped me from getting a switching and I usually ended up just having to sit on the corner of the porch.

I loved my grandmother and I knew that she loved me. I also knew that she had a softer side. So, I stopped all of the drama immediately. I was still sniffing, but I turned off the river of tears. I stood up straight and looked Aint Tankie in the eye. With a sad look on my face, I said the magical words. "I, I, I love you Aint Tankie. I love you. I really, really do. I love you." When I said this, she dropped her eyes from mine and her face softened. Inside, I felt relieved. At that very moment, I knew that I was only going to be sent to the corner of the porch to think about what I had said.

That day, I didn't get the switching that I deserved. Aint Tankie sent me to the corner of the porch to think. As I sat there, I thought long and hard about what I had said. I learned a life lesson that day. Sometimes children just need be seen and not heard. I had done something that children didn't do back then. I had crossed the line when I raised my voice and used that tone with my grandmother. I had disrespected my grandmother and I had hurt her feelings. I knew that I had to go back to her and apologize. And, I did.

In later years I realized that I got very few switchings in my childhood, even though there were times that I probably deserved one. I found out that my grandmother didn't like giving us spankings. My grandmother was a wise woman and she knew exactly what I was doing that day. The majority of the time, this wise old soul somehow managed to shrewdly turn the tables on me. She always figured out a way to maneuver things, so that I seldom got a spanking. She always left a door left open for me to use or a way out of whatever I had gotten into. In the process, I always thought that I had pulled the wool over her eyes. Now, I realize that she let me believe that my begging, crying and pleading had always gotten me out of trouble.

Some of my most precious memories are from the times I spent on my grandmother's front porch. When things weigh me down, in my mind, I still go back to my corner of the porch. When I think about that little girl sitting there, somehow my problems don't seem as bad, because I know that they too can be worked out. I can see me sitting there with my legs dangling and swinging. I see me looking across that old gravel road, over the soy bean field, to the distant interstate. I feel that warm summer breeze on my face as I breathe in all of the country smells.

While sitting there, I solved some of my biggest problems. I learned some life lessons. I learned to respect others' feelings. I grew and I changed. Each time I go back to my corner of the porch, I feel blessed to have had a loving grandmother to learn from. But something amazing also happened to me while sitting there. I developed a wonderful imagination. And, today, I realize that the foundation for most of my favorite stories was born and thought out, right there, "on my corner of the porch."

Don't Go Under The House

When I was growing up in the Missouri Bootheel, most of the houses sat on big wooden footings or cinder blocks, and so did ours. The blocks raised the houses about two feet off the ground. The breeze that flowed under each house made it an ideal place to play. But every day of every summer, when we went outside to play, my grandmother would say, "Don't go under the house."

But she never told us why! As a matter of fact, all of the adults would tell all of the kids "don't go under the house," but nobody ever told us why. We all know that when you tell a child, "don't" — in their mind, it really means "do."

The summer of my ninth birthday is when I decided that I was old enough to make my own decisions. As a matter of fact, I thought I was old enough to make decisions for me and my younger cousin, Doris Faye. I didn't understand why everybody was so worried about us going under the house. I couldn't imagine what could possibly happen that I couldn't take care of.

After all, I was nine years old; I was old enough to take care of both of us. So I decided that as soon as we got a chance, Doris Faye and I were going to go under the house and play. But just in case we got caught, I also decided that Doris Faye should go under the house first and check things out. Then, I could say, "Doris Faye did it first." I always talked poor Doris Faye into doing everything first.

Every day when we went outside to play, we would walk around the house and then we would stand back and peep under it. Each time we peeped under the house, all we saw was a perfect place to play and hide. And we saw a few chickens trying to stay cool on a hot summer day.

Every day for about a week we looked under the house and we didn't see anything but the chickens. So I told Doris Faye it was time: we were going under the house. I told her that I believed that all of the grown-ups had gotten together and made up this "don't go under the house" business. They were just trying to keep us from having fun. It had to be that, because we never saw anything under there and nobody ever told us why we couldn't go under the house.

When I was young, kids didn't ask "why," you did whatever you were told. I was different; I always had to ask "why." I would ask why, even though I knew that my mouth always got me into trouble. So, the next day I took Doris Faye by the hand and we headed for the kitchen, where my grandmother was cooking. When we got to the kitchen, Doris Faye started to slowly back up; she got behind me and peeped around my back. She was supposed to be there as moral support, but instead, she was behind me, hiding and shaking. I have to admit that I was also a little scared, so I started talking real fast. I said, "Aint Tankie, why can't we go under the house?"

When I said that, Aint Tankie stopped stirring the pot of greens that she was cooking, she whirled around and gave us that look. The first thing I thought was, Oops, I'm in trouble again ... That's when Aint Tankie said, "SNAKES!" Her loud tone caught us off guard; it scared us and caused us to jump. We had never thought about snakes being under the house. Then she added, "It's cool under the house and snakes like it. Now don't yawl go playing under there, you hear me." I looked at her and said, "Yes ma'am." We turned and ran out of the kitchen as fast as we could.

I've always been afraid of snakes even to this day, so that was enough for me, or at least I thought it was. For several days I thought about what my grandmother had said, but we had never seen a snake under the house. Then one day I decided that we were going to go under the house anyway.

The next day when we asked if we could go outside and play, we were told the same thing,

"Don't go under the house." When we went outside we walked all around the house, peeping under it at several spots. We wanted to make sure that there weren't any snakes under there and that nobody could see us. After I checked everything out I told Doris Faye, "you go under first, go just far enough to see if there's a snake under there."

Doris Faye looked at me and said, "but what if I see a snake?"

I smiled and said, "Girl, have you ever seen a snake under the house?"

She said, "No."

I said, "There's not any snakes under the house. I told you they were trying to trick us."

Doris looked at me and smiled, then said, "Okay."

Poor Doris Faye crawled under the house first as usual.

I got down on my hands and knees so that I could see her clearly, then I softly said, "Doris Faye, do you see anything?

Doris whispered, "There are not any snakes under here, but it's nice and cool."

I told Doris Faye, "Crawl a little farther and look around some more."

She smiled and said, "Okay," then started crawling farther under the house. When she was about middle ways under the house she turned towards me and said, "I still don't see any snakes."

I stood up and looked all around the house again. I was mainly checking to see if my brother and cousin were still playing by the edge of the fields. Then I ran down near the kitchen window and listened for my grandmother. I wanted to make sure that she was still in the kitchen cooking.

Once I heard her in the kitchen I ran back to where Doris Faye was. I took one last look in both directions to make sure that everyone was where they were supposed to be and couldn't see us.

Feeling safe, I went under the house. That first time we were a little scared, so we didn't stay under there very long.

After that first time, we went under the house every day for about a week. Doris Faye would go first and I would check to make sure no one could see us, then I would join her. We would play for a while, but we never stayed long and we never saw a snake. Another week passed and we still didn't see any snakes. After that we stopped looking for snakes. We were still a little afraid of getting caught by my brother, Junior and my cousin. As for Aint Tankie catching us, we really didn't want to think about the consequences. Then one afternoon my grandmother told us that she had to go into town. She said that my brother Junior was in charge.

I decided that I didn't need Junior babysitting me. I was nine years old. I could take care of me and Doris Faye. After all, I had taken care of us each time we went under the house. I was a big girl now. I didn't need him watching us. So I smiled and told Doris Faye, "Don't pay Junior any attention, just listen to me; I'll take care of both of us." Poor Doris Faye smiled and said, "Okay." Besides that, whenever my brother was in charge, he always got me into trouble and Aint Tankie usually agreed with him. I think that's why I thought it was okay to have Doris Faye do things first, in case we got into trouble. I thought it was all right to blame everything on her, the same way Junior blamed everything on me. Junior was older than me; I was older than Doris Faye, so to me it made perfectly good sense.

As soon as Aint Tankie left, Junior ran off to play in the back yard. Doris Faye and I went near the front of the house to plan how we were going to go under the house. I was trying to figure out how we could go under the house without Junior seeing us and still watch the road for

Aint Tankie. As usual, I gave very little thought to what we were about to do; then we went under the house. When we were about halfway, we stopped and looked to make sure that my brother couldn't see us. I also made sure that we had a good view of the road, so that we could watch for Aint Tankie's return.

I felt good that day because I had decided all by myself what we were going to do. I thought, I'll show them, I don't need Junior babysitting me. I'm nine years old. I'm a big girl. In my mind, I was going to show all of the grow-ups, that I could take care of me and Doris Faye. I also decided that I was going to tell them about us going under the house. I wanted them to know that they didn't have to tell us anymore, "Don't go under the house." They needed to know that it was safe to play under there.

Finally, we were having the adventure that we had waited so long for. We looked at each other and both of us started giggling at the same time. We realized that we could play freely under the house for as long as we wanted, because Aint Tankie wasn't there. I was excited. I was proud of me. I did something on my own, without anyone's help. I told Doris Faye, we can play under here for a long time today; she looked at me and smiled and said "okay." We laughed and we talked, as we crawled around in the dirt. We chased each other on our hands and knees as we kicked up dust. We had fun!

We were having so much fun that we forgot about watching for Junior, Aint Tankie, or looking for snakes. Then, all of a sudden both of us stopped dead in our tracks on our hands and knees. Directly in front of us, curled up on one of the cinder blocks partly hidden in the shadows, was a snake. It was a big, black snake and it was staring right at us. And there we were on our hands and knees and couldn't stand up and run.

We panicked and before we realized it, both of us let out this loud screeching scream. We started scrambling around so fast, that we knocked each other over. We got up and started crawling out from under the house as fast as our little hands and knees would go. I think we scared the snake also, because as we went one way, the snake went the other.

When we got close the edge of the house, we thought we were safe, but that feeling of safety only lasted for a second. Things got much worse than finding a snake. We crawled from under the house right into Aint Tankie. She was standing there with her hands on her hips. I knew that look and stance. Whenever she put her hands on her hips, she was mad and you were in big trouble.

She looked down at Doris Faye and then at me. Aint Tankie asked me, "What are you girls doing under the house?"

We said, "We saw a snake, we saw a snake."

Looking very concerned, she asked, "Are you girls all right?"

We said "yes ma'am." Then her tone changed. In a firm voice she said, "go sit on the corner of the porch."

By then my brother was standing beside her. She told him to go and get her the garden hoe. My brother ran and got her a gardening hoe. Then Junior and Aint Tankie went around to the back side of the house. They had to look for a while, but they finally found that big black snake and killed it.

While they were in the back of the house finding and killing the snake, I had time to calm down and think. In my mind, I thought, even though we had disobeyed my grandmother, we were not in any trouble. We were safe. We had not been bitten by that snake. And, if we had not found that snake, that big, black snake could have gotten into the house. I smiled and leaned back, feeling very comfortable. I had decided that everything was going to be okay, they were going to thank me and Doris Faye. So, I told Doris Faye, "don't worry, we helped them catch that snake. We just escaped death. That big black snake could have bitten us or killed us. If we had not found that big, black snake, they never would have been able to kill it." Doris Faye just sat there quietly looking up at me, and then she smiled and said, "Okay."

When my grandmother and Junior came back to the front porch, we were still sitting there. I had this little satisfied grin on my face. I was just sitting there, waiting for them to thank us. My smile was soon wiped away. Aint Tankie looked at by brother and said, "Didn't I tell you to watch these girls?"

My brother said "yes ma'am."

"Well..., what happened?"

Junior looked at Aint Tankie and said "I told them to play right here near the corner of the house so that I could see them while I pulled the weeds, like you told me to."

Doris Faye and I looked at each other. Junior was not pulling up weeds, he was playing. But we couldn't tell Aint Tankie that, because he gave her that look, and she believed him.

Aint Tankie smiled at him and said, "all right, now you go back and finish pulling the weeds." As Junior walked away he glanced over his shoulder and smiled at us. He had talked himself out of trouble again and he had talked us in to trouble. All we could do was sit there and watch him walk away.

Aint Tankie turned to us and all of a sudden she yelled, "Didn't I tell you girls not to go under the house, because of the snakes?"

She scared us and we jumped and said, "Yes ma'am."

I was just about ready to say, "Doris Faye did it first" ...

When all of a sudden ... my grandmother grabbed us and hugged us. She hugged us really tight to her chest, and then she said, "You girls are really lucky.

"Uh, Uh, Uh, you all sure is lucky today.

"Why, just the other day Fred told me about his niece. Doris Faye, she was just about your size. Why, that poor child was swallowed-up ... by a big black snake that came from, down yonder, by the river. The snake we just killed was a little smaller than that one. But, I think it was the same kind of snake that swallowed-up Fred's niece. Yes, it looked just like the snake he told me about. You girls are lucky today."

By then Doris Faye and I were scared all over again and we were crying. Aint Tankie didn't give us a switching that day. She didn't scold us and we didn't have to sit on the corner of the porch. After hearing about what had happened to Mr. Fred's niece, she could see the fear on our faces. Aint Tankie reminded us that they didn't catch that bigger black snake that swallowed-up Mr. Fred's niece. So, she told us to be very careful when we come outside to play.

My cousin Doris Faye was only five years old and Aint Tankie said that Mr. Fred's niece was about her size. We thought that if she was Doris Faye's size and that bigger black snake had swallowed her, then it could also swallow Doris Faye. After hearing all of this, we knew for sure that the bigger black snake was still out there. It was hiding and waiting for us to come out and play, so that it could eat Doris Faye.

I didn't want my cousin to be eaten by that BIG black snake. We believed what Aint Tankie said and we were afraid. So, that summer we spent the next few weeks inside. While we were inside, I did some thinking. I decided that I was not old enough to take care of myself. I decided that Doris Faye and I still needed someone to look after us. I also decided that Doris Faye and I were never going under the house again. After making all of these decisions, I told Doris Faye about them, and she smiled and said, "Okay." I took Doris Faye's hand and we went to talk to Aint Tankie.

I told her we were going to be good girls and that we were going to try to stay out of trouble.

Notice I said "TRY." After all, kids will ... be kids.

Raw Beets and Red Onions

It was late August and there were signs that summer would soon be coming to an end. Aint Tankie's day had started before the sun came up. She had gotten up early to finish picking and sorting the last of the vegetables from the garden. She had told me the day before that we were just about ready to start cooking and canning. Aint Tankie had taken some of the vegetables and made a big pot of fresh vegetable soup. It was the exceedingly pleasing smell of her vegetable soup that woke up me and my cousin Doris Faye.

As soon as I woke up, I remembered what was in store for me for the next few days. I was going to be in the kitchen, helping Aint Tankie cook and can all of those vegetables that we had picked, sorted and washed. I didn't mind working in the garden or picking vegetables, but I hated the sorting, washing and canning part. I didn't like the idea of being stuck in the kitchen for days. The only thing that made the task bearable was thinking about how good the vegetables and fruits would taste during the cold winter months.

Aint Tankie was already somewhat tired from getting up extra early that morning. So, by the time we woke up, she was already sitting on the front porch in her rocking chair. When she heard us moving around and talking inside the house, she called me to come to the porch. Since I had just gotten up, it was too early for me to have gotten into any trouble. So, my first thought was, "What did I do yesterday?"

When I went out onto the porch Aint Tankie was sitting there rocking and smiling. She said, "I have something to tell you." To my surprise, my grandmother had decided that we were going to take the day off. I was glad. We had spent the last few days picking stuff, digging up stuff, carrying stuff, sorting stuff and washing stuff. Both of us needed a break from garden stuff. I was tired of garden stuff, but I wasn't too tired to play.

My cousin had spent the night, and she needed someone to play with. After breakfast Doris Faye and I got busy playing in the front yard. We were having a fun, lazy, end-of-the-summer day, where we could play and do whatever we wanted to do all day long. Like most kids, we played for a while, then we ran out of things to do. By mid-morning we got into an argument, mainly because we were bored, so, we stopped talking to each other.

Around that same time one of our neighbors was passing by and saw Aint Tankie sitting on the front porch. He stopped and told her that Miss Pearl was sick. Aint Tankie and Miss Pearl had been friends for a very long time. She used to say, "Pearlie, I have known you since we were knee high to a duck." After hearing her say this several times, it started me to wondering what knee high to a duck meant. Well, we raised a few ducks, so I started looking at all of the ducks' legs, trying to figure if they had knees. If they had knees, I couldn't see them, so what Aint Tankie said still didn't make sense to me. So, one day I asked my grandmother, "why do you always say you've known Miss Pearl since you all were knee high to a duck?" Aint Tankie laughed and said, "Oh that just means I have known Pearlie since we were young, since we were little children."

Still smiling, my grandmother got up from her rocking chair and headed for the kitchen. She had decided to take her longtime friend some of the fresh vegetable soup she had made that morning. She asked me and my cousin if we wanted to go with her to see Miss Pearl. Both of us said "no." Miss Pearl was starting to get old and forgetful. There were times that she couldn't remember who we were. She always talked really loud, because she was losing her hearing, so we had to answer her really loud. I used to laugh at Miss Pearl because she would ask me two or three times, "Who you?" I would always answer her saying, "I'm Loretta, Miss Pearl" She would say, "ah", then turn away and say something to Aint Tankie. Then she would turn back to me again and say, "Who you?" Once again I would say, "I'm Loretta, Miss Pearl." Again, she would say, "ah." Besides that, last year they had found a snake in her house and we didn't like going there anymore.

Miss Pearl lived just down the road from us. From our front porch, if we talked loud enough, we could talk to whoever was with Miss Pearl on her front porch. For that reason we were allowed to stay at home alone. Aint Tankie told us that they would be sitting on the front porch if we needed anything. Like most kids we didn't take time to think about how close Miss Pearl's house was to our house. All we could think about was that for the first time ever, we were home alone and we were going to have some fun.

My grandmother gave us some last minute instructions and told us to stay inside, and then she left. Aint Tankie had barely made it to the gravel road when my cousin and I looked at each other and smiled. Then we ran to the front window, to make sure that she wasn't coming back. When we were sure, we looked at each other again and started giggling. We quickly forgot about being mad at each other, and we were best friends again, ready to get into something. At that time, I had no idea what we were going to do. The only thing I could think of was that we had the whole house to ourselves. We were like spies on a mission and fun was the only thing on our minds. Whatever our adventure was going to be, it had to be a good one. We were home alone and we were looking for something exciting to do.

We started in my grandmother's bedroom. The first thing we spotted was her old tin trunk, and she had forgotten to lock it. We looked at each other, then we walked over to it. We thought about all of the treasures that were inside. We thought about how close we were to all of those fun things; they were just waiting for us inside of that old tin trunk. We touched that old trunk. We rubbed the lid of that old trunk. There was something about Aint Tankie's old tin trunk that always mesmerized us, whenever we thought about what was inside. In a spellbound tone, I told Doris Faye, "all we have to do is just raise the lid up." Doris Faye looked at me.

Deep down inside of us we must have been thinking the same thing, because we jerked our hands away. We looked at each other again and slowly backed away from the trunk. As kids we got into a lot of mischief, but we were not crazy. We knew that you didn't go into Aint Tankie's trunk without her permission. That old tin trunk is where she kept every-thing. All of her possessions were in that old trunk. For us to even think about going into my grandmother's old trunk, showed that we had given little thought to our foolish adventure.

The front door was also in Aint Tankie's bedroom, which was right next to the living room. We thought about going outside, but when we peeped out of the door, we saw Aint Tankie and Miss Pearl sitting on Miss Pearl's front porch.

We quickly closed the door and decided not to go out that way. We turned around and went into the living room, but there was nothing exciting to do in there. So we quickly passed through it and into our small dining room.

The only thing in the dining room was a table with chairs, an old ice box and a shelf on one wall. On the shelf were a few dishes that my grandmother only used at Thanksgiving and Christmas. We knew that we were never supposed to touch them unless it was one of those two holidays.

Sometimes during the hot summer months we kept an ice block in the ice box. My grandmother always told us to keep the door to the ice box closed so that the ice block would last longer. But sometimes I would pull one of the chairs up to the ice box. I would open the top door where the ice block was kept, then I would put my face close to the ice block and blow on it. When I did this I could feel a little cool breeze on my face. Then I always stole a lick or two or three off the ice block. Stealing licks from the ice block always tasted better than when I asked for a chunk of ice to suck on. During the cold winter months the ice box was usually empty and the outdoors became our refrigerator. I remember my grandmother putting food into cast iron pots and then putting a lid on each pot. Then she would set the iron pots on a wooden bench that was on our back porch. The wooden bench prevented animals from getting into the food.

Other than that there was nothing adventurous in the dining room, so we headed for the kitchen.

Even though we had been told to stay inside, I decided that we were going to sneak out of the kitchen door into the backyard. There was always something fun to do in the backyard and there was nothing to do in the kitchen besides cooking and washing dishes. But when we got to the kitchen, we stopped and big smiles came over our faces as we looked at each other. We had found what we were going to do. There it was, just sitting there, waiting for us. How did we forget about all of those fresh vegetables that we been told not to touch? Unlike most kids of today, we liked munching on fresh vegetables, and there we were, surrounded by baskets and baskets, filled with all kinds of delicious things to munch on.

My cousin and I sat down and sampled a few things as we laughed and talked. We had our favorite vegetables, but we were saving them for last. Soon we were ready.

Doris and I loved sweet red beets and sweet crunchy red onions. To us these two vegetables tasted best when you took a bite of each and the two flavors blended. (Amazingly, I still like the taste of those two vegetables mixed together.) We sat there in the middle of the kitchen floor kidding around and laughing as we peeled and ate sweet beets and red onions. It was harvest time and they were perfect, they were sweet, crunchy and good.

It never crossed our little minds that what we were eating was also healthy for us. Because back then, everyone ate raw vegetables, so it was not uncommon for us to be eating them. We had eaten these vegetables and other raw vegetables many times in the past. But there was one unforeseen problem that we didn't think about that day. If you were going to eat as many vegetables as we did that day, the vegetables really needed to be cooked first. But that day, to Doris Faye and me, those sweet beets and red onions were the sweetest we had even eaten. Or, maybe they tasted so good because we were not supposed to be eating them.

It's amazing how time slips away from you when you're having fun. We sat there on the kitchen floor laughing, talking, eating, eating, and eating. Like most kids we didn't stop laughing, talking, and eating until we started to feel sick. Really sick, "green about the gills" sick. Immediately, we realized that we had eaten WAY TOO MUCH. We briefly remembered how good everything had tasted when we first sat down and started eating. The beets tasted sweet and juicy and the red onions were sweet and crunchy. But, that wasn't what we were feeling now. Both of us had that sick feeling, the one that starts in the pit of your stomach and slowly creeps back up. Next, it hits your taste buds and deep down within, you know what's about to happen. At that point, you know that you are going to throw up at any time.

We tried to lie down on the kitchen floor, hoping to slow down what was about to happen, but the kitchen kept moving and that made us sicker. The sick feeling that was rising up inside of us was indescribable. The rumbling noises coming from our stomachs confirmed it. We looked at each other and the only thing we us could say was, "I don't feel so good." The expression on our faces told the rest of the story. We were seconds from losing everything we had eaten. At that moment, we jumped up and ran out of the back door as fast as we could. We barely made it outside before it happened. Those beets and onions came way back up and they didn't taste like they did going down.

As we stood in the back yard throwing up, I felt like I was dying. I turned to my cousin and said, "Doris Faye, I think I'm dying." That's when it hit me, if I'm not dying now, when Aint Tankie finds out what we've done, I'm going to wish I was dying. I knew that there was a switch waiting for me with my name written on it. If I was fortunate enough to be sent to the corner of the porch, who knows how long I would be sitting there. My poor cousin Doris Faye always did whatever I told her to do;

now she was in trouble too and all because of me. I felt like all of this was my fault, because my grandmother had left me in charge of her. That's when I said, "Doris Faye, I think we're in big trouble this time."

We threw up for what seemed like long time. When we stopped, I think it was because we didn't have anything left inside of us. My cousin didn't look like she was feeling good and I know I didn't feel good. We sat down in the grass for a few minutes. Then we got up and went to the pump to get a cool drink of water. We were hoping that the water would make us feel better. Usually a cold drink of spring water from the pump tasted good, but that day, it only added to our misery.

We were as sick as two little girls could be, so we headed back to the kitchen door and went inside. When the screen door closed behind us, that's when we realized the mess we had made.

We stood there looking at all of those beet and onion skins. The onion skins had started to smell and our noses and stomachs didn't like it. As sick as we were, we knew we had to clean up our mess. We took everything out of the kitchen door and threw it into the grass and weeds out back. We were hoping that no one would notice or smell them. When we finished we were not feeling any better, plus we were also starting to feel a little weak and tired.

We went back inside and made our way to the living room and fell back on the couch. The rumbling noises in our stomachs started to quiet down as we sat there rubbing our tummies and moaning and groaning. We lay there on the couch thinking that nothing could be worse than the way we were feeling. That's when things got worse. We heard footsteps on the front porch and then a voice called out, "Loretta, Doris Faye, I'm back." Doris Faye and I jumped and sat straight up. Aint Tankie had returned from Miss Pearl's house.

My grandmother opened the door and walked in, then she headed straight over to where we were sitting on the couch. She had this strange look on her face as she leaned down and looked us straight in the eye. She stared at us for a few seconds then she said, "What's the matter with you girls? You all don't look like you feel good, are you sick?" We looked up at her and said, "Yes ma'am." Then she said, "What's wrong? What happened to you all? I wasn't gone long!"

At this point my cousin and I looked at each other not knowing what to say. We couldn't tell her what was really wrong with us. So we did what most kids do when they're in trouble and don't know what to do: we cried. That day that was the only thing we knew to do. As we cried we started shaking, hoping that it worked. Aint Tankie looked at us and shook her head several times. Then, her expression changed and she got this real serious look on her face that I couldn't figure out.

My grandmother shook her head again and then she said, "Uh, uh, uh, yawl don't look good, no, no, no, not at all." When she said that, I looked at Doris Faye and I could see that she was crying and shaking for real. I started to get a little worried and scared, I was wondering what Aint Tankie saw when she looked at us. Then, in a concerned voice she said, "I do believe you girls might have the sickness." I thought, "The sickness. What sickness? Why did she have to go and say that? What did she mean; we might have the sickness?" We had the same sickness that Miss Pearl had? When she said that, I joined Doris Faye, I started crying and shaking for real. Through my tears I managed to ask her, "What is the sickness?" With that concerned look still on her face, she shook her head again. Then in that sad voice, Aint Tankie said, "The sickness that's being going around, that same sickness that Pearlie got."

I didn't want me and my cousin to have anything that Miss Pearl had. Miss Pearl was old. I got so scared that I stood up and then Doris Faye stood up. At this point all of our pretend crying was long gone. We were crying for real! The only thing I could think of was that Miss Pearl was old and if she had something, it had to be bad, really bad. I was just getting ready to ask Aint Tankie again about the sickness that Miss Pearl had, but before I could speak, she spoke first. "But don't you girls worry, because I know how to cure the sickness."

When she said that, I breathed a sigh of relief. Then she said, "All you girls need is a big dose of castor oil, it's known to take the sickness away." My cousin and I looked at each other and said, "CASTOR OIL." My grandmother had said the two words that no child back then ever wanted to hear. She nodded and said, "Yep, castor oil will do the job all right. It cured Pearlie of the sickness and I know that it will cure you girls too." Like I've said before, back then most kids didn't ask "why?" They did what they were told to do. But in my mind I thought, "Why castor oil? Why can't she find something else to give us?" I almost always asked the "why" question, but that day, I was too sick to ask "why?" so I kept my mouth shut.

At this point, Doris Faye and I slumped back on the couch. The thought of taking a dose of castor oil made us feel queasy all over again. But that wasn't the end. To make matters worse, Aint Tankie told us go get the bottle of castor oil. Then, she told us go into the kitchen and get two tablespoons. We felt bad enough, having to go get the castor oil; now we had to go into the kitchen. We couldn't believe it; we had to walk past all of those beets and onions again.

But we did what we were told to do. We went and got the castor oil and took it to Aint Tankie. Then we headed for the kitchen. When we got to the kitchen door, we walked fast past the vegetables. We got the tablespoons and ran out of the kitchen. We gave Aint Tankie the tablespoons and she gave each of us two tablespoons of castor oil, to cure us of the sickness. I do believe that tablespoons back then were much bigger than they are today. As for castor oil, if you never had to take it, count your blessings. It's a nasty tasting laxative. It's clear, thick and greasy. This oily substance has a taste that is beyond words. It goes down slowly and leaves an awful taste in your mouth that lingers. One important thing to remember: do not burp soon after you take castor oil; if you do, you will experience the above symptoms all over again.

We took the medicine and both of us started to get sick all over again. We fought the reflexes to throw up. Because, if we threw up, we knew that Aint Tankie would just give us another dose of castor oil. My cousin and I didn't want that; we couldn't handle another dose. We slumped down on the couch again and after a while we were starting to feel a little better, but that didn't last for long. Our stomachs were empty from throwing up earlier and this caused the laxative to start working much faster. That afternoon I lost count of the number of times we went to the outhouse. That was one of those days that both of us were glad that we had a "two holed" outhouse.

Later that evening around suppertime, Doris Faye and I were still lying on the couch. We were starting to feel better, but we still felt a little sick and weak. Aint Tankie came into the living room and told us that she was getting ready to start supper. She looked down at us and said "I know you girls have got to be starving by now. I was thinking you girls have been through a lot today. So, I decided to fix you all something special, that I know you will like. How would you like some fried chicken with turnip greens and cornbread?" That sounded good to us, so we said, "Yes ma'am", and thank you. But, then she added, "And I think I'll cook you some of those sweet beets and maybe cut up some red onions on top and sprinkle a little vinegar over them. Doesn't that sound good?"

This time we didn't think about looking at each other for approval. Both of us said "NO!" as loud as we could, at the same time. We were hungry, but just thinking about eating more sweet beets and red onions, started making us sick and gave us dry heaves. So, for supper that night we asked Aint Tankie if we could just have a small bowl of the fresh vegetable soup she had made that morning. The soup made us feel a little nauseous, but we managed to eat it and keep it down. Shortly after we finished our soup, we went to bed and fell asleep almost immediately.

When we woke up the next morning we were feeling much better. By midday, we almost felt like our old selves again. By supper time, we were fine and ready to eat. For supper Aint Tankie fixed fried chicken and smothered potatoes with gravy and we had hot biscuits with butter. We ate a good supper. We cleaned our plates and asked for seconds on the fried chicken. Later that evening, we sat on the front porch with Aint Tankie laughing, talking and playing as usual. After a while, Aint Tankie looked at us and said "you girls ate a pretty good supper tonight." We looked at her and said "yes ma'am, it was good." Then out of nowhere she said, "I guess you girls are over all those raw beets and red onions you ate, uh?"

My cousin and I stopped in our tracks, our mouths dropped open. We didn't say a word. All we could do was look at each other. Later that evening I got up enough nerve to ask Aint Tankie how she knew what we had done. Aint Tankie looked at me and smiled as she leaned back in her rocking chair and started rocking. Chewing on her snuff brush she said, "Oh, I have a way of knowing these things." When she said that Doris Faye and I just sat there for a few minutes; we didn't know if we were in trouble or not. Besides that, we didn't know what to say or how to react to what we had just heard. That's when I realized, "grandmothers are smart people, really smart people."

Many years later, my grandmother and I were sitting on my mother's front porch. I asked Aint Tankie if she remembered when I was 8-9 years old and Doris Faye and I ate all of those beets and red onions and got sick. She smiled and said, "Yes, I remember that." I asked her how she knew what we had done. She told me, "That part was easy, you girls were so sick that day that you forgot clean yourself up."

Aint Tankie laughed then said, "You were something else when you were growing up. You were always getting into something. You used to keep me laughing and you also kept me on my toes." She sat back and looked at me and laughed again, then she said, "Sometimes I would have to turn my back, so that you and Doris Faye couldn't see me laughing. But, that day, as soon as I walked in the door and looked at you, I knew that you and Doris Fays had been into something. I could tell that you girls had been eating beets and red onions and I could also see that they had made you sick. That's when I came up with "the sickness" idea."

"You girls were so sick that you had forgotten to wash the red beet juice off your chin and finger tips. Your breath, oh; it reeked from the smell of onions and from throwing up. When I stood in front of you all and leaned down close to your face, I could barely stand the smell. You all were so sick that you didn't think about rinsing your mouths out with some baking soda and water, to kill that odor. And you, you were so sick that you were pale, your little color was almost gone. As for poor Doris Faye, she always did everything you told her to do and that's why she ended up just as sick as you."

Then, after all of those years, Aint Tankie said those two words again. She leaned forward in her chair and said, "Besides that, it was that time of the year; you needed your fall dose of castor oil. You girls needed to be cleaned out for the winter months. By getting into the beets and red onions you all made it easy for me that year. With everything that was going on I didn't have to listen to you complain about the bad taste of castor oil."

Aint Tankie told me that when she told Miss Pearl her "the sickness" story, Miss Pearl laughed and laughed for the longest time. I asked her what was really wrong with Miss Pearl that day. My grandmother said, "Oh, Pearlie, nothing was really wrong with her. She just had a touch of arthritis in her hip and couldn't walk good for a few weeks." When she told me that, I smiled and remembered what I had thought that day,

Grandmothers are smart, really smart people.

As for me and sweet beets and red onions, I didn't eat either of them for at least twenty-five or twenty six years, and that is the truth. But, these days I enjoy both in reasonable portions. I love thin slices of crisp red onions on most of my sandwiches and in my salads. As for beets, I eat them very often. I like them from a can or jar, sliced, chunks, shredded, pickled, sweet & sour, and in salads. I even like fresh beets–that is, as long as they have been cooked!

Sweet Flapjacks for Mr. Fred

I was nine years old when I started making sweet flapjacks for Mr. Fred. He had been an old and dear friend of my family for as long as I can remember. To this day, when family members talk about Wardell, Mr. Fred and his family are always mentioned in our conversations. My grandmother and later my mother would tell us the story about how our family and Mr. Fred's family came to Missouri. In the 1920's and early 1930's both families had been sharecroppers in Mississippi. Back in the early 1930's, both families had quietly slipped out of Mississippi late one night and ... well, that's another story for later.

Our families had followed each other for years, often working for the same landowners, most of those years. Mr. Fred's daughter Hester and my mother were childhood friends and remained friends. Mr. Fred's granddaughter Shirley and I were friends. Both of us attended Hodges Grade School in Wardell and we were in the same classroom. And Mr. Fred and my grandmother Aint Tankie had been friends for as long as I can remember. On holidays the two families always made sure that they visited each other's house before the sun set. The two families had been close for many years.

In the 1950's, most African Americans who lived in the Missouri Bootheel did not own property. Nor did they have much of anything else; everybody was poor. But everyone helped each other and shared what they had. If you needed repair work done around your house, someone was always willing to help you out. If someone needed a meal cooked, someone was always there to do it.

Throughout the year everyone shared what they grew and canned from their gardens. Every fall, I can remember my family and Mr. Fred's family putting their money together and buying a half or whole pig. Then they would divide the meat up equally between the two families. Then, each family would salt cure their meat to preserve it for the winter. There was always somebody with a smokehouse who would smoke and cure certain parts and the hams for the Christmas holidays.

But time changes everything and it changed each of our families also. As my mother and Mr. Fred's children grew up, most of them moved away. My mother relocated to St. Louis, but most of Mr. Fred's children moved out of Missouri. Only a couple of the older ones stayed in Wardell or other near-by areas in the Bootheel. I was four years old when my brother and I were sent to Wardell to live. But I have a lot of memories starting from the time I was five years old. I can remember Mr. Fred and his family living down the road from us. We moved and Mr. Fred and his family moved down the road from us again. When I was eight years old we moved again and Mr. Fred and his brother moved next door to us. By next door I mean a very short walking distance.

We were always at each other's house; Mr. Fred was always there for my family. He had an old T-Model car, the kind you had to use a hand crank to start. Sometimes on Saturday when we went into town for the afternoon, I can remember Mr. Fred letting my brother start the car. Whenever he did this, the next time we went into town I would always ask if I could start the car.

My grandmother, Aint Tankie would always say "no, girl you don't need to be trying to start a car." But Mr. Fred would always let me try. I can't remember ever starting it, but I always tried.

When we went into town, Mr. Fred would always give each of the kids a nickel or dime to spend and we would jump for joy. We were happy because in the 1950's a nickel or dime went a long ways. When we were in town we never wandered far, because we had to report in just like kids do today. Usually we reported in to Aint Tankie. But if Mr. Fred and some of the other older men were sitting in front of the colored people's grocery store, we would check in with Mr. Fred. To us he was family.

Sometimes when we were in town, Mr. Fred would ask my grandmother if she needed any flour or sugar. Whenever he said this, I knew that sometime during the next week, he was going to ask her if I could make him some sweet flapjacks. So whenever I heard him ask her about flour and sugar, I would smile and quietly skip off to play. But in the back of my mind I would be thinking, next week, I get to make sweet flapjacks for Mr. Fred.

When I was growing up all girls learned to cook at an early age. I liked cooking, so I didn't mind helping Aint Tankie in the kitchen. When I was eight years old my grandmother had started teaching me to cook in her old cast iron skillet. I was getting pretty good at fixing some simple things, but sweet flapjacks had become "my specialty." When I fixed sweet flapjacks for us, my brother and cousin would eat a big stack. But I always enjoyed fixing them for Mr. Fred the most. He gave me the nicest compliments as he ate each and every one of the flapjacks.

Mr. Fred would frequently come by our house to check on us and sit a spell. I can remember he used to ask my grandmother if she had any repairs that needed to be done. In an old country house there's always something that needs to be fixed. So he usually ended up repairing or replacing something. When Mr. Fred finished fixing whatever it was, Aint Tankie would always say, "Fred, what do I owe you?" Every time she asked him this, he would answer," Tankie, you don't owe me anything, but I sure would like a big stack of Loretta's sweet flapjacks."

So whenever he did any repairs, she would ask me to fix him some sweet flapjacks. And whenever I saw Mr. Fred washing up at the water pump, I knew that my grandmother was going to ask me to fix him some sweet flapjacks. So whenever Mr. Fred was nearly finished fixing anything

I would make it my business to be playing nearby. I knew that she was going to ask him "Fred, how much do I owe you?" And I knew that he was going to say, "Tankie, you don't owe me nothing, but I sure would like some of Loretta's sweet flapjacks." Whenever Aint Tankie would ask me, I would always say "Yes," with this big grin on my face.

Then we would head for the kitchen. Aint Tankie always started the fire for me in our old wood burning cooking stove. But once she got the fire just right, she would go and sit on the front porch and talk with Mr. Fred while I fixed his sweet flapjacks. I always made Mr. Fred's flapjacks in that old cast iron skillet that Aint Tankie was teaching me how to cook in. Just about everything Aint Tankie cooked or baked was in that old seasoned cast iron skillet.

We didn't have shortening or cooking oils back then; all we had was lard. Everyone used lard, which was made from frying pork fat. While the lard was melting and getting hot, I would mix the flapjack batter. When the lard got hot enough, I would pour the flapjack batter into the skillet, in saucer size circles. Those flapjacks would smell so good while they were cooking. I always let them cook until they were golden brown on both sides.

When I put the hot flapjacks on a plate, if we had any fresh butter, I would spread it on them. Before the butter finished melting, I would sprinkle each flapjack with granulated sugar. Many times all I had was sugar to put on them. But, I always made sure that I put extra sugar on all of them, because Mr. Fred used to say that he had a sweet tooth. He only had one tooth in the front, at the top, and I always thought that this tooth liked a lot of sugar.

When I took those sweet flapjacks to him on the front porch, his face would light up. Mr. Fred would sit there in the rocking chair and take a sweet flapjack in one hand and roll it up and then he would take a big bite out of it. I can remember always standing there and being nervous as I watched him eat the first sweet flapjack. But once he finished eating that first one, he would look at me, smile, and say, "These is the best ones yet." Mr. Fred always gave me nice compliments, but I liked that one the best. Then he would sit back and rock as he ate that whole stack. He would grin the whole time, smacking his lips and licking each finger after he finished each flapjack.

Once he finished the stack, a big smile would come over his face. Feeling very proud of what I had done, I would be standing there watching and waiting for that final smile of approval. His smile always made me want to make the next stack better that the last. Inside, I was always shouting, "Yes! I added the right amount of sugar for his sweet tooth."

Many years later I was talking to my cousin about Wardell and sweet flapjacks and Mr. Fred came up in our conversation. My cousin asked me about the ingredients I used. Life was easy back then and so was making sweet flapjacks. I made those sweet flapjacks with flour that had to be sifted several times, because back then flour had lumps in it. Then I added baking powder to the dry flour. Next came fresh milk from a cow when we had it; if not I used pump water. Last, I added a few fresh laid eggs straight from the chicken coop. The flapjacks were always cooked in lard from pork fat. While they were still hot, I would spread freshly churned, pure butter on them, when we had butter. Then I sprinkled them with lots of granulated sugar. And that was it.

The day after I talked to my cousin, those sweet flapjacks were still on my mind. Talking about them had brought back some strong childhood memories. I could smell and taste those sweet flapjacks. So, I decided to make me some sweet flapjacks or "pancakes" as we call them today. I wanted to fix them the same way I remember fixing them for Mr. Fred. But, due to circumstances beyond my control, I had to make a few changes or adjustments to the process.

When I was growing up in the Missouri Bootheel all we had was pork lard. Now I had to use vegetable cooking oil instead. Do they still make pork lard these days? I had to use self-rising flour, because I couldn't remember how much baking powder to use. I used eggs from who knows where or how long it had been since the chicken laid them. Today, milk is pasteurized and I only use 2% milk because the doctor says it's healthier for me. Processed butter is all you can buy today. What happened to "pure" churned butter? I had to cook my flapjacks in a Teflon skillet. We all went through the non-stick era where "the in thing" was to use Teflon, only to later find out that Teflon wasn't and isn't healthy for us. Did anyone own cast iron during the Teflon era?

The end result: I have to admit; my flapjacks didn't look, smell or taste like the ones I made for Mr. Fred. I had to throw them away. They didn't look or taste as good as the frozen ones I buy at the grocery store. I think I'm going to stay with buying and eating frozen pancakes from my neighborhood grocery store. But I will never ever forget making sweet flapjacks for Mr. Fred. I will always remember standing there nervously waiting for his smile of approval. And, that smile was always followed by "These is the best ones yet."

An Old Tin Trunk Full of Dreams

Some memories stay with us for a lifetime. Some memories seem to fade after a short time. And some memories we store in the back of our minds. Then one day something happens and they start to resurface. These memories can be so fresh that it may seem like we have stepped back in time. That's exactly what happened to me in 1991. I had forgotten one of my favorite childhood memories until my grandmother passed away in January that year. After her death I was helping my mother clean out her room and closet. In the back of Aint Tankie's large walk-in closet, I saw her old tin trunk.

Until then I had not thought about that old trunk for many, many years. I realized that day that I had forgotten about it a long time ago. Or maybe I should say, I had stored those memories in the back of my mind. When I saw that old tin trunk, I smiled, and some of my favorite childhood memories started to resurface. As I looked at that old trunk, I could see myself kneeling down beside my grandmother waiting for her to open it. I asked my mother if I could have Aint Tankies' old tin trunk. Of course she said "Yes."

As I started to go through it, I found quite a few things that I remembered from my childhood. But there was one thing in that old trunk that overwhelmed me; it was an old dress with flowers on it. That dress had belonged to my grandmother. As a child, that dress was the softest thing I had ever felt. After all of those years, I could still remember how soft it felt to my face and hands. When I was a child, I didn't know anything about the different kinds of fabric. But that day, after seeing and touching that dress again, I realized that it was made from chiffon material. Now, it was old and very fragile, but to me, it was still as soft as it was when I was a child.

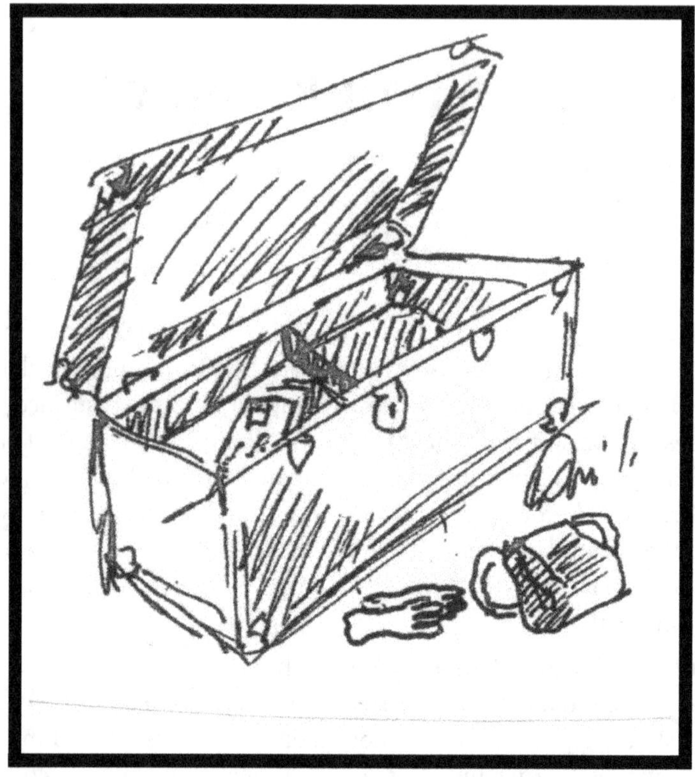

As I looked a little farther, I saw several other items in her trunk that brought back some memories. But for some reason, memories of my grandmother and that old dress kept coming back to me. The memories were starting to overwhelm me to a point that my eyes filled with tears. That's when I stopped going through the trunk and sat there with my hand resting on that old dress. My mind was flooded with thoughts about Aint Tankie. I wondered if she knew how important she was to me in my child-hood. Did she know the major role she played in my upbringing? Did I let her know how important she had been to me during her lifetime? I prayed that I had showed her through the years just how much I loved her and appreciated her. That day I couldn't continue going through her trunk, so

I closed her trunk, then left it. In the months that followed, I buried most of those memories again.

Every now and then over the next four years, that old tin trunk would creep into my thoughts. I can remember telling my mother several times that I had not forgotten about Aint Tankie's old trunk and that I still wanted it. But for some reason I still wasn't ready to continue the task of going through her trunk. My memories were starting to become somewhat bittersweet. Then, just four years later, in May of 1995, my mother passed away, and the task of cleaning out her house was mostly left up to me.

I thought that if my mother's cousin Viola, my daughter Laural and myself worked every Saturday for a while, that we would be able to clean out her house. The problem was that my mother and stepfather had lived in that house for twenty nine and a half years and they kept everything. There was so much to be done that I had to get other people to help out. With everything that was going on, I forgot to tell the young man who was cleaning out the second floor that I would take care of my grandmother's old tin trunk. So, one Saturday he emptied my grandmother's trunk.

When I arrived at my mother's house and found out what had happened, the trash had already been picked up. I was devastated. It was hard to believe that the contents of my grandmother's old tin trunk had become a part of the trash. Everything had been thrown out, including a tray that separated the top from the bottom of the trunk. This divider was about 4-5 inches deep and it separated the little trinkets that she let me play with the most.

I got a sick feeling in the pit of my stomach and it stayed with me for the rest of the day. That Saturday, as I went about emptying the kitchen cabinets, a flood of childhood memories came back to me. There had been so many things in Aint Tankie's old trunk that meant so much. All of those precious childhood memories were gone. I wanted to keep them in remembrance of my grandmother; now they were lost forever. To me, that old tin trunk was filled with priceless treasures. None of my grandmother's things had a monetary value – they were priceless to me.

I cried and cried, but once I settled down, all I could say was "I still have all of my memories." That day it didn't resonate with me that all wasn't lost. I still had her old trunk, but I had no idea how much that empty trunk would impact my life. The summer of 1995 changed my life in many ways. At that time I didn't fully understand or appreciate some of the changes. But I became a storyteller that year, and eight years later, I wrote this story.

After my mother's house was sold and everything started to settle down, I went into my office to work. I looked over at Aint Tankie's old empty trunk and it hit me just how important that old tin trunk was to Aint Tankie. Back then in the Missouri Bootheel and throughout the South, poor people didn't own very much. Being laborers or sharecroppers, they moved a lot and usually couldn't afford to buy much of anything.

Their mode of transportation was very limited and it was usually the determining factor as to what you could and could not take with you. Usually the family only had enough room to carry a few things. For that reason, the few things that you owned became more precious than gold. Their possessions were so few, that most of the time everything you owned could be kept in one trunk. And that was true in my grandmother's case. During my childhood years with my grandmother, I didn't realize that she kept almost everything she owned in that old tin trunk.

I can remember that whenever my grandmother unlocked her trunk and raised the lid, I would be there waiting. Aint Tankie would usually let me play with some of the trinkets in the tray. I was always full off questions about everything I put my hands on. Neatly folded on top in the tray, were her gloves and handkerchiefs. She had one hat and one purse, or pocketbook, as they called them back then. Her best pair of shoes was kept in the bottom of the trunk wrapped in brown paper. She wore the hat and shoes and carried her pocketbook every time we went into town. Usually, her gloves and handkerchiefs were saved for going to church or funerals.

Sometimes Aint Tankie would take the tray out and put it on the bed or floor. When she did this, she would always let me smell and put on some of her toilet water (scented and similar to, but weaker than today's colognes). As a little girl, I would open and smell all of the bottles. All of them smelled so good to me. The tough discussion was which one do I want to put on today? I usually chose the toilet water that smelled like honeysuckle. To this day I still love the smell of the honeysuckle flower.

When I tried on her hat it always fell to one side on my head. It was too big for me, but I still liked trying it on. Each time I put on her gloves, I always laughed. Her gloves always dangled on my hands, because my little fingers never reached the tips. All of her handkerchiefs had pretty multicolored flowers on them. They were soft to my skin and I always pretended to wipe perspiration from my forehead, like my grandmother did in church. I would put on her earrings while I played with her other jewelry. Some of the pieces of jewelry had missing stones, but I didn't care.

In the tray, there were odd pieces of flatware. I can remember there being some funny looking long handled spoons. I had never seen spoons like these before. I asked my grandmother what kind of spoons they were. She said, teaspoons. Then she un-wrapped a tall glass and told me it was an ice tea glass. Aint Tankie told me that she used the teaspoon and tall tea glasses for company. She smiled and said, "There's nothing like a tall glass of sweet ice tea on a hot summer day." Well, the next words out of my mouth was, "can I use one of them?" Every time I saw those teaspoons and tea glasses, I would ask if I could use one of them, and every time she would tell me, "No."

There were some mismatched water glasses that she kept for company and holidays. I thought they were the most beautiful glasses I had ever seen. They were clear glass with different kinds of colored flowers painted on them. Then, there was an assortment of other odds and ends. There were so many fun things in the tray to play with. There was enough in there to keep me entertained for hours–that is, if she had let me play with them as long as I wanted to.

But my favorite times in her trunk were when Aint Tankie would take the tray out and let me dig deep down into that old tin trunk. Right under the tray folded neatly was that beautiful floral dress that I had found after she passed away in 1991. She always carefully removed the dress and laid it to the side. Sometimes she would let me remove the dress; when she did I was always excited and nervous. It was the most beautiful and soft thing I had ever seen. When we were in what I called the trunk, in my mind this is where the real treasures were kept. In between her clothes there were colorful mismatched plates. When I got to the teacups and saucers, I would always pretend I was drinking tea or coffee. I remember asking her why she kept them under her clothes and she said to keep them from getting broken.

Folded neatly in the trunk were the few pieces of clothes that my grandmother owned. I didn't think about it then, but none of the houses we lived in had closets. Her trunk was also where she kept the few towels that she always saved for company. The only other thing I can remember seeing in her old tin trunk were small bundles of letters. Some were tied with a ribbon and some with string. They were kept neatly at the very bottom of the trunk, next to her good pair of shoes that were wrapped in the brown paper. Now, I realize that they didn't have all of today's many forms of communication. Letter writing was a large part of everyone's long distance communication. For most people back then, letters from family members were considered "precious keepsakes" and they were very important to everyone, including my grandmother.

When I think back, each time I played in my grandmother's old trunk, I would ask her questions, I asked the same questions about the same things over and over again. Like most kids, after a while I knew the answer to all of the questions before I asked them, but like most kids I enjoyed hearing the answers over and over again.

Now, there were those times when Aint Tankie would go into her trunk for something that she thought was not a child's business. On those occasions when I wanted to play with her things, she would say, in a soft voice, "Child, now you go outside and play, I need to look in my trunk."

When Aint Tankie said this, it was one of the few times that I didn't question her or ask her "why." There was something about the tone of her voice and the look on her face that told me that now was not the time to ask her "why," and I didn't. I would look at her and smile and say, "yes ma'am," then go outside and play like I was told to. I left her alone with her trunk. When this would happen, sometimes she would be in her trunk for a long time and other times it was only for a few minutes.

Back then I didn't know why she wanted to be alone with her trunk, but now I think I do. In later years I found out that it was because she was either putting money into it or taking money out of it. Somewhere in the bottom of the trunk is where she kept the little money she had. Inside three or four handkerchiefs, each tied into knots was a small roll of bills. This small roll of bills represented all of the money she had in the world. Years later I realized that my grandmother's old tin trunk was the closest she ever came to a bank.

When you have all of your worldly possessions in an old tin trunk, you are going to keep it locked. But, there was one time that Aint Tankie forgot to lock her trunk. I can still remember that day so well. I was nine years old and I thought I was a big girl. A neighbor had stopped by and told my grandmother that Miss Pearl was sick. Aint Tankie decided to take her some homemade soup and she left me and my cousin, Doris Faye home alone.

I had never been more tempted than I was that day to go into my grandmother's trunk. But without her permission, I knew better. You didn't go into my grandmother's trunk unless she told you to. If you did, she was going to find out and that was definitely a switching offense. As children, we could never figure out how she always managed to find out about all of the things that we did. I'm so glad that I didn't go into her trunk that day. If I had, I would have risked never being allowed to play in her trunk again. If that had happened, I would not have all of my precious memories to share today.

I still have Aint Tankie's old tin trunk. For years it sat under the window in my office. In 2002 I started thinking about sharing this story, because every time I looked out of the window, I looked at that old tin trunk. The memories that it brought back were so clear in my mind. Some of them were so fresh that they seemed like they happened yesterday. Precious memories that linger like that should be shared with others.

In reality, that old tin trunk has seen better days. The tin is starting to break down from age and time. It has its share of decaying rust spots. Its feel rough when you touch it. The pretty multicolored paper that lined the inside has long since faded and is starting to crumble. But, whenever I look at that old trunk, I don't see these things. In my mind, all I see is me kneeling down beside my grandmother, waiting for her to open it. Waiting to play in that old tin trunk full of dreams one more time.

The Seasoned Skillet

I was seven years old when Aint Tankie let me help her in the kitchen. My job was to wash the dishes, pots, pans and skillets. I didn't like washing dishes and I told her, but her comeback was, "Do you like eating?" Things sure do look different when you are dipping food out of a pot, compared to when you are washing that same pot. I spent the next year washing the dishes, including all of those big black heavy pots and skillets. That was my first memory of cast-iron, and that old black cast iron skillet that I would grow to love.

Most of the time Aint Tankie called her cooking utensils iron pots and skillets. At first I didn't know what cast iron was. All I knew was that everything my grandmother cooked in was black, ugly and old. It would be many years before I realized that back then, cast iron was all most people had to cook in. After you've cooked in cast iron for so long, it becomes black, ugly and old looking.

When I was eight years old my grandmother started teaching me how to cook. Since I never liked washing dishes, naturally I thought that when I started to help cook, my dish washing days would end. Not so. I enjoyed learning how to cook, but I still didn't like doing the dishes.

Aint Tankie used her cast iron daily. We cooked just about everything in cast iron, but that old heavy black cast iron skillet got the most use. At the end of the day my dish washing duties were still there, plus when I turned eight Aint Tankie added more. After my dish washing, I had to thoroughly dry all of the black cast iron pots and that old black cast iron skillet, and then I had to grease all of them with a little bit of lard. Whenever I complained my grandmother would always say, "A part of cooking is cleaning up when you're done."

My best cooking memories came from that old cast iron skillet. I remember it so well, because Aint Tankie always called it her "seasoned skillet." When she cooked in it, I only saw her sprinkle salt and pepper on the food. When we ate the foods that she had cooked in the skillet it always tasted so good. As a child learning how to cook, I watched her very closely. I wanted to see what kind of seasoning she sprinkled into the skillet to season it. But I never saw her sprinkle anything into the skillet and the salt, pepper was always put on the food before she put it into the skillet. This always left me wondering why she called it a "seasoned skillet." As a matter of fact, I never saw her do anything different to any of her cast iron.

I saw Aint Tankie cook just about everything in that "seasoned skillet." She baked corn bread in it, she baked cakes in it, she boiled in it, she smothered in it, she slow cooked in it, and she fried in it. But I always wondered why I never saw her sprinkle any seasonings in the skillet. Finally one day I decided to ask her if she ever put salt, pepper or other seasonings in the skillet and she said, "No, why would I do that?"

I said, "Don't you need to sprinkle seasonings in the skillet to season it?

She looked at me and said, "No, I just cook in it."

Well, her answer confused me even more; I still didn't understand why she called is a "seasoned" skillet.

That evening after I washed and dried the pots and the skillet, I was rubbing lard inside of them as usual. I thought, maybe this is what makes them seasoned. I went back to my grandmother and asked her, "does the pork lard I rub in the pots and skillet season them?' My grandmother said, "No baby, the pots and the skillet are made from iron and iron will rust. That's why I always tell you to dry them good before you rub lard inside of them. That keeps them from rusting." I had never seen rust on any of her cast iron, so I asked her if it was the same brown rust that I see at the water pump. She said, "yes." My grandmother must have seen the puzzled look on my face, so she added, "cooking in them is what seasons them."

Finally, I thought I knew how the skillet and the other cast iron got seasoned. I was happy until I realized that I had to keep greasing everything forever. I was hoping that one day soon, she would tell me that I didn't have to wash, dry, and grease them anymore. But she didn't, so I continued to do the dishes every day as I learned how to cook. That was my job until I was ten years old.

I returned to St. Louis to live then. By that time stainless steel and aluminum cookware were becoming popular in the city. My mother had a few pieces of cast iron, but they also looked black and ugly. I noticed that my mother always did the same thing that my grandmother had me doing. Whenever she used her cast iron she washed it, dried it, and oiled it. I never told her that greasing Aint Tankie's cast iron was my job when I was in Wardell.

Two or three years after my brother and I returned to St. Louis, my grandmother came to live with us. Guess what she brought with her? She brought that old, black cast iron skillet that I had learned to cook in. Needless to say I wasn't thrilled to see it. Immediately I asked if I could help unpack her kitchen box. I wanted to see if she had brought any other cast iron surprises.

I didn't have to wash dishes everyday like I did in Wardell. My brother and I took turns doing them, but I didn't want to start doing cast iron again. I'm happy to say I didn't find any other cast iron in her box. Through the years my mother and grandmother continued to cook in that old "seasoned skillet" when they could. But that was okay. Having to wash one piece of old heavy black cast iron was easy, compared to what I used to wash.

By the time my grandmother passed away, I was grown and married with children, and my mother was mostly using newer pots. But one day when my husband and I took the kids over to my mother's house for dinner, there, sitting on the stove with food cooking in it, was that old black cast iron skillet. I thought to myself, she's still using Aint Tankie's old black skillet. If ever there was anything that could become over seasoned, that old, ugly, black skillet had to be it. All I still saw was an old black skillet that I would have thrown away years ago.

So I asked my mother, "Why are you still cooking in Aint Tankie's old skillet?"

Mother said, "The food just seems to have a better flavor when I use it. This old iron skillet is good and seasoned now." It was then that I realized that after all those years; I was still not really sure what a "seasoned skillet" was.

So, I said, "I thought it was through being seasoned. Didn't Aint Tankie season it?"

My mother smiled and said, "It's never through being seasoned."

I thought, ah, I got her now, so I asked, "Then why do you all call it a seasoned skillet, if it keeps on getting seasoned?"

My mother said, "cast iron gets it seasoning from always being used. It gets seasoned through the food you cook in it. So the more you use it, the more seasoned the skillet becomes. And, the more you cook in it, the better your food will taste."

When my mother said this, I thought, "Now, I think I finally understand what a "seasoned skillet" really is."

So I went out and bought me a set of cast iron skillets. I was grown and married, and I considered myself a pretty good cook. After all, I had learned how to cook from the best, my grandmother and mother. Like most daughters I wanted to cook as well as my mother and grandmother, or maybe even better. In my mind the best way to accomplish this was to start out with a brand new set. My new cast iron skillets were not black and ugly-looking. Mine were grey and looked pretty. I thought, I'm not going to let my cast iron skillets get black and ugly. Then I stood back and looked at my new set of cast iron skillets. I thought, now I'm ready to start cooking like my grandmother and mother.

So I started cooking in my cast iron skillets. The first meal I cooked in my new cast iron, I had to throw it away. Everything stuck and burned. I told myself that okay, they're still new–but they said that the more you cook in them the more they get seasoned. So I believed that if I cooked in them a few times, they would be seasoned. They would soon be seasoned, just like Aint Tankie's were. So I continued to use my new, pretty grey, cast iron skillets.

My mother had a cast iron pan that had six little long slots that looked like little tiny ears of corn. She used it for baking corn bread in, so I went out and bought me one also. Oh, it was so cute, and I imagined how pretty my little ears of cornbread would look. But, guess what? I was never able to cook any of those little cute looking, perfect shaped corn bread sticks that looked like little ears of corn.

I greased the pan and they stuck. I greased it heavier and they stuck. I added so much extra oil that my cornbread was soggy and they still stuck. I even tried sprinkling a little flour on top of the oil, like you do when you're baking a cake, but everything still stuck. I tried everything, but nothing worked; everything I tried to cook always stuck and broke into pieces. I was never able to bake any cornbread in my cute little pan or bake cakes in my skillet without them sticking. I was able to fry in it, but I wanted to bake and cook other things like my mother and grandmother did. But frying in them was all I could do that wouldn't stick. Every now and then even my fried pork chops would stick.

I did all the right things, trying to make my cast iron skillets work and get seasoned and not rust. After each use I washed and dried them thoroughly. Most people didn't use lard anymore, but I found a little neighborhood store that sold it, so I bought some just for greasing my cast iron. I kept cooking, washing, and greasing my cast iron for two years. By then the grey was long gone. I had given up on keeping them grey after the first year.

After two years they were totally black inside and outside. When they turned black after the first year, I thought maybe they need to be black to get seasoned. I thought, finally they will get seasoned now. But I really didn't see much of a change during the next year. I continued cooking in them, but if it wasn't fried foods, it still stuck. Then one day, I got so frustrated after throwing away another meal, that I threw all of them in the trash.

About a week later I went over to my mother's house and there on her stove sat that old, ugly, black cast iron skillet.

I told my mother, "I threw all of my cast iron away last week."

She looked at me and said, "now, why did you do that?"

I told her, "Because I could never get mine to cook like yours and Aint Tankie's."

Well, she laughed at me, and I got mad.

With a little anger in my voice I said, "I tried really hard to get my cast iron to cook like yours and Aint Tankie's. But, I ended up throwing away most of the food that I cooked in them." She looked at me and smiled, and then she said four little words, "remember I said seasoned."

I said, "Yes."

Then my mother said "your grandmother had this skillet for as long as I can remember. I think this old seasoned skillet is older than you. She used it just about every day, year after year. So, when I got it, it was already a seasoned skillet. All I had to do was to continue cooking in it to keep it seasoned and to continue to wash, dry and grease it. It's 1992 and I bet that old skillet is at least 50 years old. It may not look pretty; it may not look grey like new cast iron, but trust me, it's good and seasoned."

Then she pointed to the skillet on the stove and asked me, "Did your skillets look this?"

I looked at the skillet and then at her and said, "no, not really, but they were black."

My mother took a sip of her coffee and sat there and smiled.

At that moment I realized that perfection can sometime take a lifetime, and it can't be rushed. What I thought I could achieve in two years had taken two generations to achieve. Finally, I think I understood what Aint Tankie was trying to explain to me that day when I was a child in Wardell. Remember my grandmother said, "Cooking in them is what makes them seasoned." But, what she didn't say was that cooking in them year after year is what also keeps them seasoned.

Now I realize what she meant, seasoned is somewhat like age. If you can weather the test of time you will be a stronger, better person. If I had taken my pretty grey skillets and continued to use them through the years, they too would have become ugly, old and black from use, but they would have become seasoned.

My mother passed away in 1995, and when I was cleaning out her kitchen, I ran across that old black, not so ugly, seasoned skillet. It brought back some memories that made me smile and cry. I wrapped it up carefully in a towel and brought it home with me. I have it to this day.

Now, I'm the 3rd generation in my family to cook in that seasoned cast iron skillet. Laural, my oldest daughter, loves to cook. I plan to pass it on to her, making her the 4th generation to use that old "seasoned skillet." Brienne, my oldest granddaughter, also loves to cook. I'm hoping that my daughter will pass it on to her. If so, Brienne will be the 5th generation to use that old "seasoned skillet." My first great granddaughter was born in June 2013. With love and care, who knows, she might be the 6th generation to own and maybe use that old seasoned skillet.

But until my daughter Laural inherits the seasoned skillet I'll continue to keep it greased. I still use that old, seasoned skillet every year. I bake corn bread in it, to use in my Thanksgiving dressing. Every year when I use the seasoned skillet, I remember my mother and grandmother. As I cook, I usually stop and take a few minutes to enjoy remembering good times and past Thanksgivings. This always leaves me feeling happy. I feel like they are always a part of our Thanksgiving Day.

To this day, once or twice a year I will pull out that old seasoned skillet and cook something in it. This may be my imagination, but I believe that the food I cook in it always tastes just a little bit better. The food always tastes like it's seasoned better than the food I cook in my stainless steel or aluminum cookware.

But after all, what can I say? It is "a seasoned skillet."

Flushing a Toilet

My grandmother, Aint Tankie, was the youngest of twelve children. One of her sisters, Aunt Pearl, and one of her brothers, Uncle Lee, lived near Wardell in Hayti, Missouri. Aint Tankie told me that I had met Uncle Lee and Aunt Pearl before, but I didn't remember it. The first time I remember meeting them, I was a very excited six year old little girl. When I think about it, just about everything excited me at age six. Our neighbor Mr. Fred always took us where we needed to go. Now he was taking us to visit with our family in Hayti. Mr. Fred had an old T-Model Ford car and I always enjoyed riding in it. Driving down the road with the windows rolled down and feeling the wind on my face always calmed me down. It often reminded me of standing in the middle of Aint Tankie's yard on a windy summer day and feeling the warm breeze on my face. The drive from Wardell to Hayti seemed like a long drive. It was long enough for me to settle down and take a nap.

When we arrived in Hayti, somebody blew their car horn and it woke me up. I couldn't believe my eyes; Hayti was much bigger than Wardell. Wardell was a small comfortable little town. Hayti was big enough for me to get lost in, and that scared me a little. We went to Aunt Pearl's house first. Later we went to Uncle Lee's and Aunt Geneva's. Whenever we went to Hayti after that we always went to Aunt Pearl's house first, then to Uncle Lee's and Aunt Geneva's house. This order continued until I returned to St. Louis at age ten. There was always more to do at Uncle Lee's house, but I still liked going to Aunt Pearl's house. I couldn't figure out whose house I liked the best.

Aunt Pearl lived on a busy street that cars were always driving up and down. There were always people out and about, walking everywhere. She lived in a brick building that had large warm rooms. I felt the heat, but

I couldn't figure out where it was coming from. The only thing I knew for sure was that she did not have a wood burning pot belly heating stove like we had. Like most kids, when you go somewhere you always have to ask for something. Since I had just met Aunt Pearl, I didn't know her well enough to know what kind of treats she had in her house, so I asked for some water.

Aunt Pearl's oldest daughter wanted to be a movie star. She wore a lot of make-up and she was all dressed up. I couldn't stop staring at her. Aint Tankie had to tell me several times to stop staring. Aunt Pearl told her to take me into the kitchen to get a glass of water. In the kitchen they didn't have a pump by the sink like our house did. Instead, there were these two little things on top of the sink and she turned one of them and clear water came running out. At Aint Tankie's house we had an old, rusty water pump by the sink that didn't work anymore. So we had to go to the pump outside. We had to prime it and pump and pump to get clear water.

Shortly after drinking the water I told Aint Tankie that I had to go and Aunt Pearl heard me. I waited for her to tell me which door to go out of to get to the outhouse. But instead Aunt Pearl told me to go down the hall. I thought the outside door was somewhere down the hall. So, I said, "yes ma'am" and headed down the hall. I was about halfway down the hall when Aunt Pearl said, "baby, don't forget to flush the toilet. I had heard some people call outhouses "toilets." But I didn't know what Aunt Pearl meant when she said "flush the toilet." So I said, "yes ma'am" and continued walking down the hall looking into each room, for the outside door. When I reached the end of the hall I looked into the last room. I saw it, not the outside door, but the outhouse, I thought. It was an outhouse toilet, but it was in the house! It was white and it had a hole in it almost like an outhouse hole, but this hole had water in it.

I walked into the room and I saw a big white bathtub and a white bowl on the wall. I remembered seeing a bathtub that looked almost like this one at the picture show in Wardell. But I didn't know what the white bowl on the wall was for. And, I still couldn't figure out why the outhouse toilet was sitting on the floor with water in it. Where did the water come from? This outhouse had everything in one room and all of it was white and shiny. I was used to outhouses sitting outside, away from the house. Aint Tankie's outhouse was just an old wooden outhouse with a wooden bench that had two holes cut into it. If you moved around too much on the bench you got splinters. Aunt Pearl's outhouse toilet was sitting on the floor in a room. I was in shock. They had a fancy outhouse in the house and it had its own room.

Now, I really did have to use it, but I wasn't sure how to use it. It took me a few minutes to figure out what to do next. All three of these things had those little handles on them just like the sink in the kitchen. When my cousin turned the handle on the sink in the kitchen, water came out of it. Maybe these little handles turned also. I gently tried to turn the handle on the outhouse toilet the same way my cousin did with the kitchen sink. It moved a little, but nothing happened. I tried turning it again, this time a little harder than the first time. Then all of a sudden I heard this loud gushing sound. I jumped back and peeked into the outhouse toilet. I think I did what Aunt Pearl had told me to do. I had flushed the toilet!

I stood there and watched the water swirl around and around in circles and then disappear. Then the water came back and it was clear and clean looking. I thought to myself, so this is what happens when you "flush the toilet." In the excitement, I forgot that I really did have to use it, but I soon remembered. I quickly used it, and then I turned that little handle again and flushed the toilet. I watched the water swirl around and around again and disappear. I stood there watching and waiting. I wanted to see if it was going to come back clear again, and it did.

I walked over to the bowl on the wall and it had two little handles on it. There was a piece of soap lying on the rim of the bowl. The soap smelled just like the summer flowers that Aint Tankie had in her yard. Still curious, I decided to turn one of the handles on the bowl. I was amazed when warm water came from it. I picked up the soap and rubbed it between my hands. I put my hands under that good feeling warm water and watched it run through my fingers and into a little hole at the bottom of the bowl. I looked under the bowl to see if the water was running out on the floor, but it wasn't. I wondered where it went, just like I wondered where the outhouse toilet water went.

I dried my hands on my clothes as I stood there, looking all around the room. I was overwhelmed by everything that had just happened to me. I was happy, excited, in shock and tired. I think I was tired because I had learned so much since we got to Aunt Pearl's house. I couldn't handle learning any more right now. I needed to rest for a while. I walked out of the outhouse room, but I stopped in the hallway. I looked back into the outhouse in the house, still feeling confused.

I walked back up the hall to where everyone was sitting. I was tired, but I was feeling very proud about what I had learned. I quietly sat down like any other expert toilet flusher would do. But inside I was beaming with joy and I was a proud six-year-old. I had learned so many new things already that I couldn't imagine learning any more that day. I sat there wishing that Aint Tankie had a toilet at her house, like the one Aunt Pearl had. But if we ever got one, it didn't have to have a room of its own like theirs. I just wanted one that we could flush.

Shortly after my new adventure ended and I had settled down next to Aint Tankie, I started to doze. My grandmother woke me up and we said our goodbyes and left Aunt Pearl's house. We headed for my first visit to Uncle Lee and his wife Aunt Geneva's house. When we left Aunt Pearl's house, I thought we had another long drive ahead of us. I was still tired and thought that I had time for a nap before we got there. We drove a short distance, then we made several turns. I was just starting to doze when Aint Tankie said, "well we're here," and we were at Uncle Lee's house.

Uncle Lee and Aunt Geneva lived in a wooden house, but their house was not as old as Aint Tankie's wooden house. Scattered here and there on the same road were a few other wooden houses like theirs. Next door to their house was a big cotton gin that had three buildings. The pipes from the cotton gin were running everywhere into the other buildings. There were a few other smaller buildings nearby and a few more down the road. When we got out of the car the first thing I noticed was two pecan trees and a walnut tree in Uncle Lee's yard. Later Uncle Lee told me that when the pecans and walnuts come in season, that I could have as many as I could carry.

When we went inside of their house, everybody was smiling and hugging each other. Uncle Lee and his wife kept saying how happy they were to see us. They gave me a big hug and said how much I had grown. Then they offered me some hard candy from a glass bowl that was sitting on the table. I sat down and I could feel the heat from the big pot belly stove that sat in the middle of the room. That pot belly stove made Uncle Lee's house feel more like home. At Aunt Pearl's house, I could feel the heat, but I kept asking myself where it was coming from. I liked Aunt Pearl's house, but I liked Uncle Lee's house more, because it reminded me of Aint Tankie's house. It was small and made of wood and it had land all around it. The yard was big enough to play in and there were a lot of interesting things to do in the front and back yard.

From where I was sitting I could see that they had a sink in the kitchen with two handles on it. The handles looked just like the ones at Aunt Pearl's house. This made me wonder if they had an outhouse toilet in the house also. I had to find out. So, when I saw their sink I immediately asked for a drink of water. Aunt Geneva told me to get a glass off the counter and get some water from the sink. Even though I had never gotten water from a sink before, I remembered how my cousin did it. I proudly got up to go get my water when Aint Tankie asked me, "do you know how to do it?" I thought, why did she ask me that? I bet she don't know how to use the outhouse toilet. I looked at my grandmother and smiled, then said, "I know how."

I got a glass and took it to the sink and then I turned the handle. My glass started to feel warm and I got scared, I thought where is this warm water is coming from. I turned the handle back and poured the warm water out.

I stood there thinking, why is the drinking water warm? Again, I thought about when we were at Aunt Pearl's house. When my cousin got me a glass of water, it was cold. When I washed my hands in the outhouse in the house, it was warm. Why? I stood there looking at the sink and the two handles, trying to figure out why the water was warm.

Finally, I decided that maybe I should try the other handle. I slowly turned the other handle, I waited for my glass to feel warn again, but instead it felt cold. I let out a sigh of relief; I filled my glass with cold water and drank it. When I finished, I started thinking, how did they make one handle with cold water and one handle with warm water? Looking puzzled, I thought, how can both of them come out of one hole? I had learned something new, but I didn't understand it. I kept thinking how did they do that? I was standing there trying to figure it out, when Aunt Geneva asked me if I was okay in there. I said, "yes ma'am, I'm okay." I put my glass into the sink and with unanswered questions still in my head, I headed back to where they were sitting.

I sat down still wondering how they make one handle with cold water and one handle with warm water. I was thinking deeply about water, when I felt the urge to go. I leaned over and told Aint Tankie that I had to go, bad. She asked Aunt Geneva if I could. Aunt Geneva raised her hand and pointed and said, "why sure, it's right in there." I jumped up and thought, "Yes!" I knew that they had one in the house. There it was right there, next to their bedroom, an outhouse in the house. It had an outhouse toilet with water in it also. It had everything in it, just like the one at my Aunt Pearl's house.

I used it and I flushed it as I'd done before. I stood there and watched the water swirl around and around and disappear. Then it came back clear, just like at Aunt Pearl's house. I remembered what to do next. I walked over to the bowl on the wall and washed my hands. Once again, I proudly walked back into the room and sat down. Smiling inside just like I did at Aunt Pearl's house. I had learned something else. This reinforced what I had said about Aunt Pearl's outhouse in the house. I really wanted an outhouse toilet in Aint Tankie's house.

I enjoyed my first visit to Hayti. I had learned a whole lot about out-houses in the house, toilets with water in them and handles that made cold and warm water. When we left Hayti, I still had some unanswered questions about where the water came from and where it went. But, as soon as I got into the car, I went to sleep almost instantly. I was still tired from learning. The next few times we went to Hayit, I spent most of my time drinking water and then going to the "toilet." (As you can see I didn't say outhouse toilet, I simply said "the toilet.") This was always followed by washing my hands with warm water.

It didn't matter whose house we were at. It was fascinating watching the water swirl around and around and then disappear. Then it would re-appear clear and clean. As for the warm water, I never figured it out, I just enjoyed it. Also, as curious as I was, I never did figure out what happened to the water when I flushed the toilet. I often wondered where that water went. How did it disappear, and then re-appear clear and clean?

My grandmother never did get an outhouse toilet. Each time we went to Hayti, it always amazed me, that their outhouse had its own room, inside of the house.

Raining Cats and Dogs

In the 1950's the Missouri Bootheel land owners usually provided houses for their laborers to live in. All of the houses usually had tin roofs. It didn't matter if we were on the porch or inside the house, the sound of raindrops hitting the tin roof always rang out loud and clear. Whenever we had a hard rain, the raindrops always played a tune on the tin roof and sometimes we would sing along with it. But, whenever we had a slow steady rain, when the raindrops hit the tin roof, the sound they produced was calming and very relaxing. This calming sound always made us drowsy and when this happened, we knew that a nap was coming.

The last thing we wanted to do on a summer afternoon was sleep. The only thing we wanted was for the rain to stop so that we could go back to playing. Like most kids, when we had those relaxing and calming summer rains, we fought the urge to take a nap. Also like most kids, when my brother Junior and I had to sit still for a period of time we always got a little antsy. This was always followed by an argument. Our arguments were usually about nothing, so we forgot most of them afterwards. But on those rainy days when we argued, we usually ended up being chastised by our grandmother, Aint Tankie.

My grandmother always said that her bones told her when it was going to rain. She always said that she liked smelling the wet earth when it rained. (To this day, whenever it rains and I smell the wet earth, I always think about her.) So on this particular day, when the rain started, Aint Tankie was already sitting on the front porch. She was sitting in her rocking chair, rocking as she chewed on her snuff brush. We knew that she was just waiting to see what our restlessness would lead to, before she stepped in. We knew that trouble awaited us if we argued, but we argued anyway. Aint Tankie calmly continued to rock as our voices get louder and louder. When we were on the verge of screaming at each other, we knew that Aint Tankie was going to stop us. Because this is what she always did. Then, in a firm voice, slightly louder than ours, she was going to say, "y'all stop all that fussing! You hear me?"

The rain continued and Junior and I continued to argue, but Aint Tankie didn't intervene; instead she continued to rock. After a while Junior and I looked over at her. At any time now, we were expecting her to say, "y'all stop all that fussing! You hear me?" But, she didn't stop rocking and she didn't stop chewing on that old snuff brush. Our argument got louder and louder and then the screaming started. When that happened, all of a sudden Aint Tankie stopped in the middle of rocking.

When she stopped rocking, she was leaning forward in her rocking chair. We looked at her and then at each other and thought that was strange. Then all of a sudden Aint Tankie looked up through the rain, at the dark sky. But she didn't look at us or say anything to us. Junior and I looked at each other again. Our expressions showed that we were thinking the same thing. Why did she stop leaning forward in her rocking chair? Why was she getting her face wet? Why was she looking through the rain at the dark clouds? Then all of a sudden Aint Tankie said, "nope, I don't see one." Then she leaned back into her rocking chair and started rocking again.

A few minutes later she stopped rocking again in the forward position. Again we wondered. Why did she stop, leaning forward in her rocking chair? Why was she getting her face wet? Why was she looking through the rain at the dark clouds? After staring at the clouds for a few seconds, again my grandmother said, "nope, I don't see one," then added, "I thought for sure I heard one this time." She leaned back in her rocking chair and started rocking again like nothing had happened. This time she rocked for about a minute, and then she stopped in the forward position again.

As kids, all this starting and stopping and leaning forward looked kind of funny to us, so we started laughing. But we still wondered. Why did she stop, leaning forward in her rocking chair? Why was she getting her face wet? Why was she looking through the rain at the dark clouds? Then she started talking again, "nope, I don't see one. But, I know I heard one this time. I heard it as clearly as could be. I know I heard it!"

She leaned back in her rocking chair and started rocking again. But we didn't laugh this time. This was not the Aint Tankie we were used to. We got scared and we started wondering if Aint Tankie was alright. We looked at each other and started whispering. "Is she all right? Is something wrong with her? What should we do? I don't know what to do, do you? Do we need to go get Mr. Fred?" Then Junior said, "maybe we should ask her if she's okay before we go get Mr. Fred."

By now we had forgotten about our argument and being mad at each other. We were worried about our grandmother. So, we decided to ask Aint Tankie if she was all right. I told Junior, "Go on, ask her." Junior said, "No, you ask her." We went back and forth a few times about who should ask her. While we were still trying to decide who would ask her if she was alright, Aint Tankie stopped rocking again in the forward position. She leaned forward in her rocking chair getting her face wet, then she looked through the rain at the dark clouds. While looking up she started talking to herself again, "I still don't see one. But I'm sure I just heard both of them clearly. I know what I heard!"

I was ready for us to go get Mr. Fred, but Junior decided that he would ask Aint Tankie if she was all right. Junior got up and went over to Aint Tankie's rocking chair. He stood there for a few seconds then he softly said, "Aint Tankie are you alright?" She looked at him and said, "did you hear that? Don't you hear the cats and dogs? I don't see them, do you see them?" Junior looked at me puzzled, then he turned to Aint Tankie and said, "no ma'am, I didn't see any cats and dogs." I could tell that Junior was getting nervous. Aint Tankie looked all around her, then she looked at Junior again. With a worried expression on her face she said, "they say that when we get a hard rain like this one, that it rains cats and dogs."

Looking shocked and confused, poor Junior said, "what?" That's when Aint Tankie chuckled, and then she let out this big belly laugh. Junior looked at me for a second, confused, then both of us remembered that old saying and we started laughing also. We had heard it at least a hundred times. But when Aint Tankie started acting strange and saying strange things, raining cats and dogs, never crossed our minds. I didn't tell Junior, but I remember thinking, "I should've remembered. I should have known what she was doing." The summer before, I had gotten my face wet a few times looking for cats and dogs.

All we could say was, "Aint Tankie!" We realized that she had gotten us again. Then all three of us started laughing again and we laughed until we cried. When we did stop laughing, Aint Tankie looked at us and grinned. The next words from her mouth were, "I stopped you two from arguing, didn't I?" Then, she smiled and started rocking and chewing on her snuff brush. By now, the rain had stopped. I had a smile on my face, but inside I was still laughing. All I could think about was how smart Aint Tankie was and how she had gotten us again.

Today, all of my grandkids are grown, but there are times when we reminisce about when they were growing up. They often ask me, "Nan, how did you always know what to do when we argued?" When they say this, I simply smile and say, "you all couldn't fool me, I have been there and done that, long ago when I was your age. Your great grandmother, Aint Tankie was an expert at figuring out how kids think." To this day I have to admit that there are still times when I wonder, "How did she know what I was going to do?"

The Making of Sweet Peach Juice

I was cleaning out my pantry and I ran across my grandmother's old stoneware crock. I pulled it out and picked it up and started to examine it. This started me to thinking about some of my childhood memories that involved that old crock. Around the outside, printed in rather bright blue ink, was the number 3. Below the number 3 in the same bright blue ink was printed Ruckel's Stoneware. I turned it over and engraved on the underside was Ruckel's Pottery and the year 1870. Under 1870 was the name of a town in Illinois called White Hall.

I remember smiling and thinking, I never thought about that old crock being a 145 years old. The outside had a few battle scars and several cracks. The underside was not glazed and the hard clay was exposed. In researching the crock, I learned that back then they didn't glaze the undersides. The rest of the inside and outside surfaces were glazed. The glaze still had a shine in it and it was in very good condition. Again I thought, this old crock is over 145-years old, "WOW." More memories of my grandmother, Aint Tankie using it came to mind. But, I still wondered about the year and decided to check into it.

I found out that the crock was not over 145 years old. The 1870 date on the underside was the year Ruckel's Pottery was established in White Hall Illinois. Ruckel's marked the undersides of their crocks before glazing them. The year 1870 engraved on the underside was introduced in 1920 to mark the 50th Anniversary of Ruckel's Pottery. Today Ruckel's Pottery pieces are collectible, and I believe that my grandmother's crock is at least 70-80 years old. But as I was gathering this information, I realized that the age and money value were not equal to the precious memories that I had of that old crock.

One of my fondest memories of my grandmother's crock was the year of my tenth birthday. It was also the last summer I spent in Wardell. Later that year my brother, Junior and I returned to St. Louis. Every summer I spent in Wardell was always filled with fun, excitement, exploring and getting into trouble. It was a hot, humid, rainy summer afternoon when my brother and I got into trouble over the sweet peach juice. We were playing in the yard and the clouds kept coming and going, covering the sun. My grandmother was doing what she usually did on days like this one. She was sitting in her rocking chair, rubbing her shoulders and knees. Then she started predicting what the weather was going to do. As usual, she said that we were going to get some rain that day. Even though she was right most of the time, I didn't want to believe that it was going to rain that day. I was having too much fun playing. So I giggled and whispered to Junior, "there she goes again." Junior looked at me and laughed.

Soon after we laughed at Aint Tankie, the clouds moved in, and this time they didn't go away. Then the rain started and we ran for cover on the front porch, Aint Tankie was right again. We sat there and convinced ourselves that this was just a rain shower and that it would be over soon. We wanted to go back and play but the rain kept beating down on the tin roof. We were very familiar with the sound that rain made when it hit a tin roof and we didn't like it. It was usually a peaceful sound that had musical notes woven into it. But it was also a hypnotic sound that lured you in. If you weren't careful and you listened to it, you were asleep in a few minutes. I knew this for a fact, because more than once I had let myself be lured into the tune the raindrops played on the tin roof.

I wasn't ready for a nap that day, so I tried to tune out the sound on the tin roof. I stood up. I sat down. I crossed my legs. I straightened them out. I looked over at Junior. He was yawning. I knew that it was just a matter of time before he drifted off to sleep. So I leaned over and nudged him. He roused up and said, "leave me alone." Soon after I nudged him, there was a loud clap of thunder, followed by a big flash of lightening and I got scared. I looked at Aint Tankie. The thunder and lightning didn't bother her; she was starting to doze. I turned to Junior who was still yawning and said, "wanna have some fun?" His stopped yawning and said, "what?" I said, "come on, you'll see." I looked back at my grandmother and she was asleep.

We quietly got up and tiptoed across the wooden porch to the front door. We very slowly and quietly opened that old squeaky front door and went inside. Then we slowly closed the door behind us. Both of us were laughing softly and we were telling each other sshhhhhh. When we got to the living room, we looked out of the front window; Aint Tankie was still sleeping. Once we saw that she was still asleep, we let out a little laugh. Junior asked me what we were going to do. I told him, you'll see. We hurried through our small dining room and into the kitchen. Then I stopped. Junior looked at me and said, "Loretta, what are you up to?" I looked at him and I said, "want some sweet peach juice?" and I pointed to Aint Tankie's crock. His mouth dropped open. With disbelief written all over his face he quickly said, "No! Are you crazy! I'm not gonna touch Aint Tankie's peach brandy."

For as long as I could remember, every summer my grandmother made "peach brandy." Every year she always told us not to touch it. I had listened to her say time and time again, "don't y'all bother my peaches in the crock." Year after year I obeyed her and didn't touch, stir, smell or taste her peaches while it was making peach brandy. Every year I watched her get everything ready and put it into the crock, so I knew what to do and how to do it. When I turned 9-years old last year, I was a big girl. I was old enough to stir and taste her old peaches.

She always used the peach skins and the peach seeds that were left over when we canned peaches for the winter months. Then she added some kind of spices that always made it smell good. She always added a lot of water, almost to the top of the crock. The last thing she added was sugar, lots and lots of sugar. With all of that sugar in it, I knew that it had to be good. The sugar is what started me to calling it sweet peach juice. She had a large wooden spoon with a long handle on it. The spoon always lay beside the crock. Once a day when we were in the kitchen cooking, she would take the wooden spoon and stir the crock then taste the mix. To me, it seemed like the stirring and tasting went on forever.

I told Junior about when I first tasted it. One day when I was alone in the kitchen, I stirred the crock and tasted the mix. Shocked, he looked at me and said, "What?" I told him that it was kind of bitter and I frowned a little. I didn't know what it was supposed to taste like, but it didn't taste bad and it didn't taste good. But I had decided that I didn't want to taste it anymore. Then I told him, "but Aint Tankie kept stirring and tasting it day after day." Then, one day she tasted it and said, "it's getting there." I wondered what she meant by it's getting there, so I decided to stir the crock and taste it again. This time the bitter taste was almost gone. It was a little strong, but it was sweeter. I smacked my lips and thought, "not bad," and then I said, "it's getting there." After that, I started tasting it every day I got a chance to. Just like Aint Tankie, whenever I tasted it, I always said, "it's getting there."

Then I told Junior that a few days ago Aint Tankie stirred the crock and tasted the mixture and said. "it's getting there, it'll be ready soon." Later that day when I got a chance to taste it, it was good as usual to me, so I said, "it's getting there." I didn't really notice a difference in the taste, but I did know that it was sweet and good. The next day Aint Tankie said the same thing when she stirred the crock and tasted it. I knew then that it would be gone soon. So I asked Junior again, "do you want some sweet peach juice?" This time he slowly said, "maybe I'll taste it." I knew that Junior would like the sweet peach juice if he tasted it. So, I grabbed the wooden spoon and stirred the crock, then I tasted it, and it was still good. I stirred the crock again and got another spoonful and said, "here Junior, try it, it's good, it tastes like sweet peaches."

Junior tasted it and frowned, and then he said, "this is good!" I looked at him and smiled, and then I said, "I told you it was good." We laughed, then I stirred the crock again and both of us had another spoonful of sweet peach juice. We stopped laughing long enough to listen for the rain on the tin roof. We could still hear it, but it wasn't as loud. We tiptoed into the living room and peeked out the window at Aint Tankie; she was still asleep. So we headed back to the kitchen for another spoonful of sweet peach juice. I stirred the crock again and had another spoonful and then Junior stirred the crock and had another spoonful.

We looked at each other and laughed again. I looked at him and said, "it tastes just like sweet peaches, don't it?" Junior looked at me and nodded and then he laughed again. I told him, "sshhhhh, you're going to wake up Aint Tankie." We laughed again, and then we quietly tiptoed to the living room window again. It was still raining, but we could barely hear it on the tin roof, and Aint Tankie was still asleep. After three spoonfuls each of peach brandy we were feeling pretty good. But we decided to have one more spoonful before we went back on the front porch.

I stirred the crock and had one last spoonful, and then Junior stirred the crock and had a spoonful. We looked at each other and laughed and laughed. We tried to stop each other by saying sshhhhhh. But, for some reason washing that wooden spoon was so funny. We started laughing again, even louder. Again we tried to stop by saying sshhhhhh to each other. Finally I finished washing the spoon and I laid it back by the crock. We tiptoed back through the dining room into the living room. We didn't bother to stop and look out the living room window, because we were headed for the front door.

After four spoonfuls of sweet peach juice, we forgot about the squeaky front door. So, when we got to the front door we pulled it open as usual and it squeaked as usual. The squeaky sound woke up Aint Tankie just as I stepped onto the porch with Junior right behind me. She looked at us and immediately asked us, if we were going into the house or were we coming out of the house.

I said we were going in and at the same time Junior said we were coming out.

My head cleared up long enough for me to think, it's over. After two years of stirring that old crock and sipping that sweet peach juice, Junior got me caught.

The look on our grandmother's face told me that she knew everything. In a loud clear voice she said, "what y'all been into?" We tried to straighten up long enough to say, "nothing," but before we could, Junior laughed and I giggled. Aint Tankie looked at us and said, "what's funny?"

Besides the smiles on our faces, neither one of us could think clear enough to answer her. Then, she said, "why y'all smiling? But before we could answer that question, she immediately asked us, "have y'all been in my peach brandy? Her question got our attention and we looked at each other, trying to think. But before we could think, Aint Tankie asked, "are y'all tipsy?" By then, we realized that she was asking us questions faster than we could answer them. We didn't know what to say or do, so we just stood there. The only thing we knew for sure was that Aint Tankie was mad.

Aint Tankie told us to sit down and be quiet. She told us not to move or say a word until she decided what to do with us. We did as we were told. We sat down and we were quiet. I remember sitting there thinking, no more sweet peach juice. Then I looked down and discovered that we were sitting on the edge of the porch. Our legs were dangling over the side, but they were dry. I looked up at the sky and the rain had stopped. Then I said to Junior, "the rain stopped." I laid back on the porch with my legs still dangling and I looked up at the tin roof.

The next thing I remember was waking up and smelling the fried chicken. Aint Tankie was fixing supper and it was dark. Junior and I had fallen asleep on the porch and Aint Tankie let us sleep there. I woke Junior up and we went inside. Aint Tankie didn't say a word to us, she just kept cooking. Later that night after supper, Aint Tankie told us what our punishment was. We couldn't do "anything" for the next three weeks.

That following morning my grandmother said that the peach brandy was ready. By that afternoon she was straining it. Before the sun set that evening, she had poured all of the sweet peach juice into jars and sat them on the eating table. The next morning when we got up, they were gone. There were no signs of that year's peach brandy. She had gotten all of it out of the house, somewhere between sunset and sunrise. The crock was washed and packed up with that wooden spoon and put back where she kept it. If she kept any of the peach brandy for herself that year, we never saw it.

The Devil Beating His Wife

Now that I am a grandmother and great grandmother, I understand a lot of my grandmother's old sayings. But one that I never understood as a child, was about the weather and the rain. Right before she would say, "it's gonna rain today," she would look up at the sky. If she was sitting in her rocking chair she would always rub her knees. If she was standing she always rubbed her shoulders. Either way, looking up at the sky and rubbing her shoulders or knees was always followed by, "it's gonna rain today." There were times that she could even predict whether or not we were going to get a light rain or a heavy rain.

Sometimes when she said this I would look up at the sky, but I never did see anything. Then, I would think, it's not going to rain today. I can't count the number of times I said this, only to be wrong. If Aint Tankie said it was going to rain, chances were it would rain. After a while I learned to hate whenever she start rubbing her shoulders or knees. I didn't want to hear those dreaded words, especially if I was playing and having fun. But, I had learned that every summer in the Missouri Bootheel we always got a few long, hard summer rains. When the rains came, we had to stop playing. We either sat on the porch or we went inside and looked out of the window or the door at the rain. That is, except for the summer we were permitted to go out into the rain and listen to the devil beat his wife.

One day we were playing outside and our grandmother was sitting on the front porch in her rocking chair. She looked up at the sky and rubbed her knees and said, "it's gonna rain today." Then she added, "it gonna be a hard one, cause the sun is shining." Soon after that it started to rain and she told us to come on the porch. I was having fun and didn't want to stop playing. When my brother ran past me he said, "come on, Loretta." I rolled my eyes at him and got up. By the time I reached the porch, I was mad. My brother tried to tickle me and I whined and said, "stop." He said, "what's wrong with you?" and he tried to tickle me again. This time I yelled, "STOP." He stopped and looked at me and shrugged his shoulders.

Then I started to cry because he was ignoring me. Aint Tankie said, "Loretta, stop all that crying, ain't nothing wrong with you." I stopped crying, folded my arms, stuck out my lip, put on my mad face and started pouting. A few minutes later my grandmother looked over her shoulder at me and smiled. She turned back around and started rocking. Then, out of nowhere she said, "did y'all hear that?" Junior immediately said, "what?" She said, "there it is again, did you hear it that time?" Junior said, "no ma'am, I didn't hear anything." Aint Tankie looked over at me and said "Loretta, did you hear it?" I said, "no" and continued to pout. I was curious, but I was still trying to pout and not show my curiosity.

Aint Tankie turned back around and acted like she was listening for something. Shortly after that she turned around again and said, "there it is again, y'all don't hear that." I couldn't hold it any longer. Junior and I asked her, "hear what, what is it?" Aint Tankie beckoned for us to move closer, then she said, "come over here and sit beside me and I'll tell you what I'm hearing." By now she had our attention. We wanted to know what she heard, so we moved closer to her. With a serious look on her face, she looked at both of us. Then, she leaned forward in her rocking chair. In a soft voice, just a little higher than a whisper, she told us this little short story. They say that when it's raining and the sun is shining, you can hear that old devil beating his wife.

Leaning back in her rocking chair she said, "I think I just heard them." They say that if you want to hear them better, you got to put your ear to the ground. Then you can hear them good. Now, if y'all want to hear them better, you have to go out in the rain and put your ear to the ground. Aint Tankie leaned back in her rocking chair and started rocking and said, "Yep, that's what they say." Both of us sat there, getting anxious. We wanted to hear what the devil sounded like when he beat his wife. Junior and I looked at each other, but I have to admit I was a little scared. We had always been taught that the devil was not good. But I really wanted to hear it.

I can still see my grandmother's face and her expression as she told us this story.

Aint Tankie told us that if we promised to be careful, she would let us go out into the rain and listen to the devil beat his wife. But she said that if the sound got really loud, that meant that they were getting closer. She told us that if that happened, we needed to run back to the porch as fast as we could. We said, "yes ma'am," then I asked her, "can we do it, can we do it?" At the same time Junior was saying, "please, please Aint Tankie, can we?" With a worried look on her face, Aint Tankie slowly said, "well, okay." Then she added, "but I don't want y'all to listen too long; it's dangerous." We quickly said, "we won't." We got up, beaming with excitement as we ran out into the rain with the sun shining. We couldn't wait to hear the devil beat his wife.

We were so excited that we forgot to ask her where in the yard. So, there we stood in the middle of the yard, in the rain, looking all around. Finally, we said, "Aint Tankie, where should we go?" She smiled and said, "anywhere is fine, right there is a good spot." So, my brother and I got down on our hands and knees in the rain. Then, we put our ears on the wet ground. The rain continued to come down on us as we laughed. I forgot about being mad, I was having too much fun. As the rain continued to pour down on us, we listened closely, hoping to hear the devil beating his wife. I remember raising up and saying, "Aint Tankie, I can't hear anything," and my brother saying, "me neither." Still sitting in her rocking chair, rocking with a smile on her face my grandmother said, "keep on listening, you'll hear him."

Well, Junior and I stayed out there until we were soaking wet and our ears were full of mud. Finally, Aint Tankie said, "maybe he didn't beat her today. We'll just have to wait for the next rain when the sun is shining. Y'all come on back on the porch and dry out. We didn't want to stop listening, but then Aint Tankie said again, "come on back on the porch now, so you can dry out." Wet and muddy, we finally gave up that day and went back on the porch to dry out. In the past, I had never noticed the sun shining when it rained. But after that day I had a reason to listen to my grandmother when she said it was going to rain, especially if she said that the sun was going to be shining. That summer it rained a lot while the sun was shining, or maybe I just noticed it more.

Regardless, each time it rained and the sun was shining, we always begged Aint Tankie to let us go into the rain and listen to the devil beat his wife. When she did, we always put our ears to the wet ground to listen.

We always stayed out there until we were soaked and she made us come back to the porch. We really believed that the devil beat his wife when it rained and the sun was shining, and we wanted to hear it. One day it started to rain, but it was cloudy, then the sun came out. Aint Tankie gave us permission to go out into the rain and listen. We ran off the porch to the middle of the yard; we got down on our hands and knees and put our ear on the wet ground.

We listened and listened. I was thinking, we're not going to hear him again today. Then, I heard something. I pressed my ear harder to the ground and I heard it again. I screamed, "Junior, Aint Tankie, I hear him, I hear him. I hear the devil beating his wife. Junior, don't you hear him?" Junior said, "be quiet! I can't hear anything with you yelling." I put my ear to the ground again while Junior was trying to hear the devil. I wanted to know what they were saying. But a few seconds later a little smile came over Junior's face and I knew what it meant. Then with excitement in his voice he said, "I can hear him, I can hear him." When Junior said that, I forgot about trying to understand what the devil and his wife were arguing about. I jumped up and ran toward the front porch yelling, "Aint Tankie, we heard him, we heard the devil beating his wife."

Aint Tankie was sitting there calmly rocking, chewing on her snuff brush. Our faces were lit-up with excitement and we were grinning from ear to muddy ear. A big smile came over Aint Tankie's face, and then she said, "I told you, I told you that you could hear him. Uh ha, you heard him didn't you? We looked at each other, then back at Aint Tankie and nodded, "yes ma'am." Then all of a sudden, the three of us started laughing uncontrollably. We had heard the devil beat his wife!

Summer was almost over the second time we heard the devil beat his wife. I was excited and I tried again to understand what they were saying, but I couldn't. But, once again we ran and told Aint Tankie that we had heard them again. This time when we told her she smiled and said, "sho' nuff," then all of us started laughing. In the excitement I forgot to ask her if she knew what they were saying.

I was seven years old that summer and I believed just about everything I was told. Later, when the leaves were falling and it was turning cold, we got some rain. The sun was not shining, but I thought about the devil beating his wife. Most of the things that had excited me that summer didn't anymore. But I never did understand what the devil and his wife were saying. I went to Aint Tankie to ask her, but she didn't answer me. Instead she started talking about Thanksgiving and Christmas. I soon forgot about the devil beating his wife. The holidays were coming and I was getting excited.

The next summer I was eight years old and I had become a big girl, or so I thought. My younger cousin Doris Faye spent some time with us that summer and I had someone to play with and to look out for. I was past being the spoiled little sister who needed everyone's attention or else I pouted. As a big girl, I knew everything. I had all of the answers to all of my problems. So that summer when Aint Tankie said that her bones hurt and that it was going to rain, I just looked at her. When the first warm summer rain came and the sun was shining, I just looked at it. I shrugged my shoulders and quietly mumbled, "I guess the devil going to beat his wife today," and I continued playing with Doris Faye. Junior had also moved on to new adventures, with our other cousin. That whole summer neither one of us talked about the devil beating his wife. And we really didn't want to put our ears in the mud.

We never really talked about the devil beating his wife again, but I thought about it. As I got older I used to wonder sometimes what we really heard. What convinced us that we were hearing the devil beat his wife? Two years later when I was ten years old, my brother and I returned to St. Louis. A few years after our return to St. Louis, Aint Tankie came to live with us. She didn't want to leave Wardell, but things were changing in the rural south. Field work for laborers was starting to decrease, because machines were picking the cotton that laborers once did. Plus, it was the late 1950's and Aint Tankie was getting older. She had a few friends left in Wardell, but not any family members. This worried my mother, so she asked her to come live with us. I was happy, because I was still having problems adjusting to the city schools and I missed Aint Tankie and Wardell.

When Aint Tankie first arrived in St. Louis I couldn't stop talking. I had missed her. I didn't give her much time to be alone, I was always nearby and usually talking. One day we were sitting on our city front porch and Aint Tankie rubbed her legs and said, "my bones ache, I think it gone rain." Sure enough, about thirty minutes later it started to rain and the sun was shining. When the rain hit the concrete pavement, it made a sound just like the one we heard, when the devil beat his wife. I looked at the hot, dry pavement and watched the steam rise from it. I thought about Wardell. I remembered how dust rose from the hot, dry ground, when the rain hit it. I got excited and said, "Aint Tankie, that sounds just like the devil beating his wife."

When I said that, Aint Tankie's face lit-up and she started laughing. I asked her what was funny. She looked at me and said, "Oh, I was just thinking about the first time I told you and your brother about the devil beating his wife. That saying had been around for years, I don't know where it came from. Everyone used to say it whenever it rained and the sun was shining. You all never wanted to stop playing and come in when it started to rain and you always got mad. That day I told you and Junior that story, I thought you would just laugh about it. I didn't think you would believe me, but you did. You stopped pouting and you and your brother got so excited. I played along, thinking that surely one of you would catch on anytime, but you didn't."

"So I sat there and watched the two of you have one of the best rainy afternoons you ever had. But it didn't end that afternoon. I couldn't believe that it lasted all summer. I didn't know what I was going to do, if you all didn't hear the devil beat his wife before it got too cold to put your ear to the ground." Both of us laughed and then I quietly listened as Aint Tankie finished telling me how we'd come running, sure we'd heard him. Afterwards I smiled, slumped down in my chair and closed my eyes, and recalled that day. I remembered the smell of the dirt when the rain first hit it. I listened to the raindrops and remembered the sound. That day, after talking with Aint Tankie, I chose to continue believing that the sounds we heard were the devil beating his wife. Even though I never understood what they were saying.

I was fortunate to have had a grandmother like Aint Tankie. She gave a spoiled seven year old little girl one of her favorite childhood memories. And she did this one rainy day when the sun was shining. Who would have thought that getting on your hands and knees and putting your ear in the mud could be so much fun? After all, one summer in Wardell, I heard the devil beat his wife, two times.

To this day, if I'm around someone and it rains and the sun is shining,

I always say, "the devil is beating his wife." A lot of people have never heard this old saying. I always smile and tell them Aint Tankie's little story and how I got an ear full of mud one day when it rained and the sun was shining.

Greenwood Cemetery

Haints in the Graveyard

A few weeks after I turned eight years old, we were playing outside of the school during the morning at recess. I sat down in the grassy area between Hodgen School and the little church that sat next to it. As I sat there looking at the church I started thinking about the revival meeting that was there the week before. I started smiling because I thought about my brother and how he tried to get religion during the revival. But, instead of getting religion he ended up getting in trouble with Aint Tankie.

I sat there by myself giggling, because my brother was in trouble instead of me. I thought about how I was always the one who ended up being sent to the corner of the porch. Junior was older than me and he usually managed to talk his way out of whatever it was. But not that time. Still smiling, my eyes slowly wandered from the back of the church to the front.

My eyes stopped at the small graveyard that sat in front of the church. I sat there staring at all of the wooden grave markers and the sandstone headstones. Every day I came to school and every time we went to church, I passed that little graveyard, but I never paid much attention to it. But, now when I passed it, I looked at it differently. Now I wondered, do those graves have haints in them?

Shortly before my eighth birthday Aint Tankie moved into a house that had an old graveyard in the field behind it. My grandmother told us time and time again not to go into the graveyard. Whenever we asked why, the answer was always the same. In a loud voice she would say, "didn't I tell y'all that there's haints in there?" Those words usually ended the conversation. Aint Tankie's words had started me to wondering about haints. They made me want to go into the graveyard and find a haint.

I was eight years old and I thought I was a big girl. I was tired of everybody always telling me not to do this and not to do that. I thought that I was old enough to go into that old graveyard, if I wanted to. I wanted to see a haint, and I wanted to know more about them. But I was too scared to ask my grandmother any questions.

One morning I woke up feeling brave. I decided that I was going to ask my grandmother to tell me some more about haints.

That afternoon Aint Tankie was sitting on the front porch, so I went and sat down beside her. I talked with her for a while, then I said, "Aint Tankie, tell me some more about haints." Before she could answer me I asked, "What do haints look like? Will they hurt me? Are they as tall as Mr. Fred?" Aint Tankie just sat there quietly rocking. When I finished with all of my questions, she stopped rocking. She leaned forward in her chair and gave me that look. Calmly, she said, "if you go in that graveyard, you'll find out." That's all she said, then she sat back and started rocking again, and I got scared.

The adults had told all of us kids pretty much the same thing about haints, but none of us had ever seen one. We had talked about slipping into the graveyard and finding some haints, so that we could see what they really looked like. I believe all of us were a little scared of that old graveyard, even though none of us ever admitted it. So we never went into it. But now I was ready. I was determined that I was going to see a haint that summer and I knew that I could handle it, because I was a big girl.

I told my cousin Doris Faye about me going into the graveyard to look for haints. When I said the word haints, Doris Faye got scared, but I told her that she was too young to go. When I said that her expression changed, she smiled and looked relieved. I told Doris Faye that I would tell her all about the haints, but not about the scary stuff. Since Doris Faye was too young to go with me, I decided to ask my brother Junior and our cousin to go with me.

Soon after I told Doris Faye about my plan, I started remembering more and more of the scary stories they had told us about the haints in the graveyard. All that thinking about haints scared me a little, but I was still excited about finally seeing one. But the more I thought about it, the more I kept putting off asking my brother and cousin to go with me. I didn't tell Doris Faye or anyone else, but all of that thinking about haints made me dream about them.

So, before the end of summer, I decided that I didn't have time to go looking for haints. I told myself, next year for sure.

During the fall and winter months, we had our usual cold rains, cold weather and snow. Sometimes when the weather got really bad, we couldn't go outside and play. During those times I always walked from room to room looking out of each window. I always seemed to end up looking out of the back window in the bedroom we slept in. I would stand there staring across the field at the large cluster of trees where the graveyard was. My thoughts were always about all of the haints that were in there. I noticed that during the winter months the grown-ups didn't talk too much about the haints. So, this made me wonder if haints ever showed themselves when the weather was cold.

Finally, winter was almost over and the weather was starting to get a little warmer. I turned nine years old that year, but before my birthday I had already decided that I was going to see a haint that summer.

A few days after my birthday, Mr. Fred came by our house. He wished me happy birthday and he told me how much I had grown in the past year. When he said that, a big grin came over my face. Then, he added that I was becoming a big girl. My grin faded. I thought, I'm already a big girl.

The warmer weather also meant that the teachers at school let us go outside to play. As soon as we came out of the front door, we started running and chasing each other around the school building. When we ran past the church I looked over at it. When we got to the graveyard, I stopped and I started thinking about haints. I realized that I wasn't as scared as I was the year before, when I was only eight years old.

All winter, I had been looking out of the back window of Aint Tankie's house at that old graveyard. I remember standing there thinking, this summer I'm finally going to see a haint. I was ready, I was excited and I had a plan. I didn't know when, but I knew that it was going to be before fall. We just had to wait for Aint Tankie to leave the house long enough for us to go into the graveyard.

Doris Faye was still too young to go with me. So, one day I asked my brother if he and our cousin had ever been in the graveyard. He said, "no!" I told him I wanted to go see a haint and I asked him if they wanted to come with me, and he said "no!" I told him that he was scared and he said, "no I'm not." I said, "yes you are". I told him that the only reason I asked him was because Doris Faye was too young to go with me. I smiled, and then I said, "well I'm going, but I just thought that it would be more fun if the three of us went together.

After all of that, he still told me no.

My brother's final no made me more determined. I knew that Junior never liked missing out on anything. So, that's when I told him that I was going to ask our cousin to go with me. Junior still tried to act like he didn't want to go, then he said, "okay! I'll go." I looked at him smiling, but he didn't know how glad I was that he had said yes. I wanted my brother to be with me when I saw my first haint.

After Junior said yes, I said that I didn't believe haints were as scary as we had been told. I looked at him with conviction, as I told him that we were going to prove it. That summer the three of us were going to show all of the grown-ups that we were not afraid of an old haint. I told him that we had to do it when Aint Tankie wasn't around. Even though I had convinced him to go with me, I knew that he could change his mind. If he did, I wasn't going to see a haint that summer, because I wasn't going into that old graveyard by myself.

One afternoon Mr. Fred stopped by our house to see if Aint Tankie needed anything done. I heard Aint Tankie tell Mr. Fred that she didn't have any work for him that day. Then, the two of them went and sat on the front porch and continued talking, laughing occasionally. I quietly went and stood by the side of the house and eavesdropped on their conversation.

I had gotten mad when I heard Aint Tankie tell Mr. Fred that she didn't have any work for him. I started pouting, then I mumbled, "if she doesn't have any work for Mr. Fred, I guess I don't get to fix him sweet flapjacks today." I was nine years old and I still liked fixing sweet flapjacks for Mr. Fred. I really liked fixing them now, because earlier that year things had changed.

One day I was making some sweet flapjacks for Mr. Fred, when my grandmother told me to start making enough batter for all of us. That day I was grinning from ear to ear as I thought, I got to make sweet flapjacks for everyone. Mr. Fred was always stopping by asking Aint Tankie if she had any work for him. For a while she always had something for him to do. I forgot that a time would come when she didn't have any work for him. On those occasions, none of us got any sweet flapjacks.

I think my teeth had become sweet teeth, just like Mr. Fred's sweet tooth. Both of us liked extra sugar on our flapjacks. But, that afternoon my sweet teeth were not going to get any sweet flapjacks. While I was standing there pouting and eavesdropping on their conversation, I heard something I wasn't supposed to hear. I knew that I wasn't supposed to listen to grown folk when they were talking, but it was fun. Besides, Aint Tankie was always telling me to stop talking so much and listen sometime. So, most of the time I didn't call what I was doing eavesdropping. I was listening.

While I was listening that day I heard Mr. Fred say, "Tankie, you not gone believe what I saw yesterday in the afternoon." I leaned closer to the wall, then I peeked around the corner. I wanted to make sure I could hear what he had seen that afternoon.

Mr. Fred leaned forward in his chair. Aint Tankie stopped rocking and she leaned forward in her rocking chair. Then Mr. Fred said, "I saw a haint in that old graveyard back yonder." My grandmother said, "sho' nuff Fred." Mr. Fred nodded and said, "sho' nuff, Tankie." Aint Tankie said, "uh," then leaned back and started rocking again.

When I heard Mr. Fred say that he had seen a haint yesterday, I jerked my head back. I stood there shaking. I wanted to run but I couldn't, I wanted to hear more. I thought, maybe today I can hear some more about haints. So, I leaned closer to the wall and peeked around the corner again. Then Mr. Fred said, "I didn't know they came out in daylight, but there it was, standing there in that old graveyard, in broad daylight." Aint Tankie shook her head and said, "well I declare! In broad daylight, Fred?" Mr. Fred said, "yep, in broad daylight. If this one did it, that properly won't be the last one we'll see in daylight."

Aint Tankie looked at Mr. Fred and said, "Fred, what do haints look like in daylight"? Mr. Fred shook his head, then he said, "one night I was walking down the road and I felt one touch me. Tankie, it scared me, oh it scared me so bad that I jumped and started running as fast as I could down that road." Then he stopped talking and started shaking his head again. After a while Mr. Fred continued, "I thought being touched by one was scary, but seeing one in broad daylight is worst. Tankie, I am a man and it give me the chills."

After being quiet for a while Mr. Fred said, "it was scary, real scary. If they come out in daylight, who knows what they gone do next? I sho' hope none of these kids ever see a haint in daylight or be touched by one." All my grandmother said was "uh, uh, uh." I thought, as long as I can remember, I can't ever remember Aint Tankie being lost for words.

I stopped eavesdropping; I turned around and ran as fast as I could to the back of the house. I sat down between my brother and our cousin. Then I scooted close to my brother. A little cool breeze was blowing where they were sitting. I needed that breeze because I was hot, scared and breathing hard. As I sat there, I stared at that old graveyard. It looked so peaceful, sitting there in the middle of the field. Then I remembered what Mr. Fred had just told Aint Tankie. I thought about how bored we had been this summer, waiting for Aint Tankie to go somewhere. Now, I was thinking, are we really ready to go into the graveyard?

Finally I started to cool off, calm down and breathe normally again. But I wasn't my usual talkative self. I sat there, still and quiet, staring at that old graveyard. I was tempted to tell Junior and my cousin what Mr. Fred had said. Then I thought, if I tell them they won't go with me. As we sat there leaning against the back wall, I kept thinking, what should I do? I was scared, but I still wanted to go into the graveyard. But I also couldn't stop thinking about what I had just heard.

Once again, I wasn't sure if I was ready to see a haint this year. Maybe I should wait until I turned ten years old. I sat there and stared and stared at that old graveyard. In the back of my mind, I was hoping that I would see a haint then and there in the daylight, just like Mr. Fred did. I thought, if I see a haint right now, then we won't have to go into the graveyard. I sat there quietly for so long that Junior nudged me and asked, "what's wrong with you?" I quickly said, "nothing," and then I moved over a little, still quietly staring at the graveyard.

I stared for the longest time and I didn't see a haint or anything else moving over there. Then it hit me. I couldn't see anything because the sunlight was so bright that it was blocking my view. Mr. Fred saw the haint in the graveyard when he was walking by it. I needed to be closer if I wanted to see a haint. I could hear those old familiar words echoing in my head, "don't yall go in that old graveyards back yonder, it got haints in it." I tried to convince myself that what we were doing was okay.

Mr. Fred had seen a haint and we wanted to see one also, but we didn't know what to do if we ever saw one. The grownups told all of us that if we ever saw a haint to never look it in the eye, but they never told us why. They said that haints would hurt us, but, no one told us how to protect ourselves. When we asked what a haint looked like, they just shook their heads and said, uh, uh, uh. They said that they made these strange noises, but nobody ever told us what the noises sounded like. They always told us that they smelled really bad and if we ever smelled one, we would remember it. Sometimes for no reason, Aint Tankie or Mr. Fred would say, "do you smell that? I think a haint is close by." Whenever they said that, we would get scared.

We had our own version of what we thought a haint looked like and smelled like. We thought that all of them were big and tall. They staggered when they walked, but they could run really fast. We didn't know what a haint sounded like, but we were convinced that we would recognize the sound if we ever heard it. As for the way haints smelled. The worst smell we could think of was the outhouse in the summer. No haint could smell worse than that. All of us wanted to see a haint, but we knew not to look it in the eye, because if you did, well ... We really didn't know what would happen, but it had to be something bad. For that reason, we knew that you should never look into haints' eyes.

By the afternoon I had talked myself back into wanting to see a haint. I had convinced myself that we were not breaking Aint Tankie's rule. We were not going into the graveyard. We were just going near the graveyard. That was safer, in case we had to run in a hurry. I also convinced myself that I was ready, at nine years old, because I was a big girl.

I decided that we needed to do it, as soon as the time was right. I also decided that I didn't have to tell my brother and cousin everything I had heard that day. I did tell them that Mr. Fred had told Aint Tankie that he had seen a haint in broad daylight. They asked me what else he said. I told them that he didn't say anything else about haints and that they just talked about grownup stuff.

A few weeks passed by before the time was right. Then, one day Aint Tankie told us that she was going into town to pick up a few things. Mr. Fred was taking her, so she told us that we didn't have to go with her to carry the bags. She told us that she wouldn't be gone too long. By the time she finished telling us what to do and not do and what to eat if we got hungry, Mr. Fred was there. So, she hurriedly told us that Miss Pearl was right down the road if we needed anything. When she told us all of this we knew that we had enough time to go to the graveyard. The day was perfect, it was hot and sunny, just like the day Mr. Fred saw a haint in that old graveyard.

As soon as Aint Tankie and Mr. Fred left, we slipped out of the back door so that Miss Pearl couldn't see us leave. We ran as fast as we could across the open field and out of Miss Pearl's view. When we got near the old graveyard we stopped. We were hot, sweaty and out of breath, but we were three very excited kids. That day we were going to see our first haint. We were going to prove to everyone that we were old enough to handle seeing a haint. We stood there near the graveyard in the hot sun, trying to see into the graveyard, waiting to see a haint.

We stood there in the hot sun for what seemed like a long time. We stared at the trees, trying to see beyond them, but we couldn't, because they were loaded with leaves. The harder we looked, all we saw was more trees covered with leaves, and we couldn't see anything. We heard ruffling sounds coming from the graveyard and we looked at each other with fear. We didn't know if it was a haint, the wind or what. I was ready to run back to the house, but I couldn't let my brother and cousin see my fear. This was my first real adventure with the boys, and I missed Doris Faye. So, I stood there and waited for them to do something first.

Finally, my cousin said, "we need to get closer." I shook my head, but my brother said, "okay," so we moved a little closer. My brother said, "Loretta, are you sure Mr. Fred saw a haint in daylight?" I said, "yes, I'm sure." So, we stood there for a while, not saying a word and not seeing a haint. Then, my cousin said, "let's go in; we need to go into the graveyard to see a haint." My brother looked at me and said, "Loretta, do you want to go in?" I hesitated too long in answering and the adventurous boy in my brother came out and he said, "okay," and started walking. He looked back at me and said, "come on, I don't see anything."

I went into the graveyard with my brother and cousin. They didn't stop moving once we got inside the graveyard. I could tell that they were excited and having fun as they looked all around. They were laughing and talking about how the graveyard looked. As for me, with every step, I shook harder than before. I couldn't help showing some of my fear, but I tried hard not to show all of it. I knew that if they saw how scared I was, they would tease me forever. I tried to catch up with them, but they were walking too fast and I couldn't. As scared as I was, I thought, maybe I should have told them that the haint Mr. Fred saw was in this graveyard.

The deeper we went into the graveyard the more shaded it became. I wondered where the sun had gone; I needed to see the sun. The sounds we had heard while standing outside of the graveyard were now mixed with others that I had never heard before. I listened to all of those unfamiliar sounds as they got louder and louder. I was hearing all kinds of noises. I started thinking; one of them had to be the sound a haint makes. Before I could finish my thought I started to smell some dampness. Another, unfamiliar smell mixed with the damp. My first thought was, that's what a haint smells like? I was getting more and more afraid that what I smelled was a haint. I thought, if one of them is near me, I hope it don't touch me.

My heart was pounding. I could hear the strange sounds that haints made and I could smell them all around me. I knew they were there.

Then, I remembered that I shouldn't look them in the eye. So I shut my eyes and started running in the direction of my brother and cousin. All of a sudden I started falling. It felt like something had grabbed me by the leg and was pulling me down. I knew that a haint had grabbed me. I had been touched by a haint! It was scary just like Mr. Fred said. I could hear my heart beating in my chest, but I kept my eyes shut. I had changed my mind. I didn't want to see what a haint looked like.

I was shaking all over. With my eyes still shut tight, I started screaming. I remember thinking, what's going to happen to me, why didn't they tell us what to do? Then I heard my brother calling my name. He was telling me to stop screaming before Miss Pearl heard me. Then, he said, "Loretta, open your eyes, open your eyes." When I opened my eyes, Junior was standing over me holding onto my arm and my cousin had my hand. They were trying to keep me from falling into a hole. I looked down just long enough to see that I was on one knee and my other leg was in a hole. Then I felt them jerk me up real fast.

They asked me if I was okay. But, before I answered them I looked all around me to make sure the haints were gone. Then I said, "did you see where they went? Are you sure they're gone? Where did they go?"

Junior and my cousin looked at me and said, "ain't nobody here but us, there ain't no haints here." I said, "yes there are, I felt one. It touched me." They told me several times that there weren't any haints in there. I still didn't believe them. One had touched me. Then they finally said, "okay, okay, the haints are gone, now let's get out of here. We got to get back to the house before Aint Tankie and Mr. Fred."

The three of us started running out of the graveyard as fast as we could. When we reached the fields, we forgot all about Miss Pearl seeing us. We just ran.

When we got back to the house, Aint Tankie wasn't there yet. We had lost track of time in the graveyard; we were not gone as long as it seemed. All of us had enough time to wash off the mud. I was still shaking as I washed the mud off me. I wondered what I had fallen into.

While I was washing up I heard my brother and cousin laughing. I got mad and mumbled. When I finished I asked them what they were laughing about. I knew they were laughing at me because I'd screamed. They looked at each other and started laughing again. My next thought was, they saw a haint and won't tell me what it looked like. So, I said, "you all saw a haint, you saw one– didn't you?" They laughed and said, "no, we didn't see a haint." Very calmly my brother said, "Loretta, there ain't no such thing as a haint. We just wanted to have a little fun with you. We wanted to scare you, but we didn't want you to fall like that, you could have hurt yourself. We just wanted you to stop bothering us about going into the graveyard to look for haints. "

When my brother said that, I got mad and said, "yes there is, there's haints in that old graveyard!" That's when I told them, "Mr. Fred saw one in there, in broad daylight a few weeks ago. Mr. Fred wouldn't say that if it wasn't true." Then Junior and my cousin got mad at me, because I didn't tell them that the haint Mr. Fred saw was in that old graveyard. All of us liked Mr. Fred, and whatever Mr. Fred said, we believed it, because Mr. Fred said it.

When Junior and our cousin found out that Mr. Fred had seen a haint in that graveyard, they changed their minds. They knew that if Mr. Fred said he saw a haint in that old graveyard, in broad daylight, it was true. Then they believed me. I didn't look that haint in the eye, but I had smelled it and it had touched me. And I know that it was a haint that was pulling on my leg. I told them the reason they didn't see the haint was because I was running behind them.

They'd been having so much fun that they didn't turn around to check on me until I screamed. By then that old haint had disappeared and went where haints go in the daylight. But I could still smell it and I think I heard it make a sound. After what Mr. Fred said, I told them, they better be glad that they didn't see it. I'm glad I kept my eyes shut and didn't look at it. I had felt a haint touch me and just like Mr. Fred said it was scary. I don't want to think about what would have happened to me if I had opened my eyes.

For the rest of the summer, Doris Faye and I found lots of things to do together. I never told Doris Faye about that day because I didn't want to scare her. For some reason the three of us never talked about our adventure in the graveyard that day and we never told Aint Tankie. My brother and my cousin believed me when I told them everything Mr. Fred said. Knowing that Mr. Fred and I had been touched by a haint was good enough for them. As for me, after that day I never got the urge to go back into that old graveyard again and I never wanted to see a haint.

That was the only adventure I had with my brother and cousin. I decided that I didn't like doing things with the boys. I didn't like them taking charge and telling me what to do. Yes, they looked out for me and helped me when I was in trouble. But I missed my little cousin and I missed being in charge and taking care of me and Doris Faye. I decided that we didn't have to play with the boys to have fun.

I was in my teens when I found out why all of the adults told us all of those haint stories. The stories were all made up because of the sunken graves in graveyards. Back then, over time, graves would sink down as much as one and a half or two feet, and if you stepped in one it could sink even more. The adults were worried that one of us might fall into a grave and get hurt or worse. So, in an effort to keep the kids out of the graveyards as much as possible, the adults came up with the haint stories. To this day I don't know what I stepped in back then. All I know is that it was muddy.

As for the day I eavesdropped on Aint Tankie and Mr. Fred – I didn't know that they'd seen me standing there, peeking around the house listening to their conversation. So, as they talked, they made up the story about seeing a haint in that old graveyard in broad daylight. Aint Tankie told me that I had talked so much about that old graveyard and haints that they wanted to scare me. They were hoping that it would make me not want to go in there. Their story did scare me, but only after I went into the graveyard. After my grandmother told me the truth about their haints story, I still did not tell her about that day.

Everyone always knows when I attend a burial. They hear me as we walk to the grave site. They hear me as we stand at the gravesite during the actual burial. That's because as I tip toe and dance my way between and around the graves, I'm constantly apologizing to the deceased, saying, "ouch, ouch, I'm sorry."

To this day whenever I go a cemetery I don't like stepping on graves. I don't even like accidentally stepping on the edge of anyone's grave. When I accidentally step on a grave, I am so remorseful that I feel led to say, "I'm sorry" at least five or six times. For years after I became an adult, whenever I accidentally stepped on a grave, my apologies were out of respect, and out of fear of what might happen.

Do I still believe in haints? Well ...

Running Up the Wall

In 2003 I went back to Wardell to take pictures of the town and the surrounding areas. I drove down the road where I thought my old school was. I couldn't believe my eyes when I saw the old building. I had attended Hodgen Grade School from 1951 to 1955. Through the years I've dreamed about Hodgen. I didn't expect for it to be still standing, but there it was. This small, four room brick school building had always felt comfortable and safe to me. When I returned to St. Louis in late 1955, the schools were extremely different. I remember being overwhelmed by the size of the city schools. I was also amazed to see that there was only one grade in each room.

In Wardell we always shared the room with another grade. That was the norm back then and we always got along. Each grade only had a few books and supplies and we shared them also. We ate lunch together in the classroom and when the weather was nice, we ate outside on the grass. At recess and lunchtime we took turns on the swings and we played games. Everyone got along with each other most of the time. At eight years old, two of my favorite things to do at recess were playing on the swing and learning how to run up the wall.

The swings were fun and I loved to ride them, but there were a few problems. Our one and only swing set only had four seats, and one of them was always broken. This meant that at recess, if you didn't get there first, chances are you weren't going to get a chance to swing that day. The teachers never monitored the swings, so we didn't have a time limit. This meant that if you got there first you could swing until your legs got sore from the wooden seats or you got tired.

Some of us were fearless and we always tried to go as high as we could. Our goal was to swing as high as the swing set was tall. With wooden seats, in order to swing that high we had to do a lot of what we called pumping. Going forward, we'd stretch ourselves backwards like a plank, and going backwards, we'd hunch forward, knees and calves gripping the wooden seat. Pumping was fun, but it came with a price. The splinters from the wooden seats could cause sores in the bend of the back side of our legs. When this happened you were out of commission for a few days or a week until your wounds healed.

A few times I managed to swing as high as the swing set was tall. Whenever this happened I always got some sores. But I was proud of my scars, even though I was in pain and healing for about a week. I can still remember the flying feeling I got every time I went up that high. I would lean back in the swing until all I could see was the blue sky and feel the wind on my face. It felt like I was soaring like the birds that flew above me. After a while of pumping and gliding, I would start to slow down; at this point I would sit up so that I could stop. By then my legs were sore and I couldn't do it again. But that didn't stop me from seeking out other adventures.

One day at school I saw some boys playing a game on the side of the school building. I went over and watched them for a while, then asked them if I could try it. They stopped and looked at me and laughed and then several of them said, "no." My feelings were hurt as I stood there and tears started to swell up in my eyes. My brother, Junior was in the group that laughed. He looked at me and said, "girls can't play this game and they can't run up the wall." I got mad and turned and walked away.

I went to the front corner of the school building and sat down in the grass. I never told my brother that I cried that day. As my tears started to subside I started thinking, I'll show him. That was the day I decided to learn how to play the running up the wall game. The next day I got a chance to try running up the wall. I recall admitting to myself that it did look like it was hard. Then I remembered that those boys had told me I couldn't do it. I was determined I was going to show them that I could.

I was scared at first, then I tried running toward the wall, but I stopped before I got to it. That's when I realized: it was hard.

I thought, this is a stupid old game. Those boys are crazy, I don't know if I really want to try it. I wish they had never told me no and just let me try it.

Somehow, at that moment I knew that I was going to learn how to run up the wall. I had to show those boys that I could. I wasn't thinking about what would happen if I collided with that brick wall or how badly I could get hurt. The only thing I was thinking about was I'll show them that I can too run up the wall.

It took me a week before I got up enough nerve to try it again. Then one day during recess, the boys were off doing something else and nobody was playing by the side of the building. This was my chance. I walked over to the wall; I peeped around the corner to make sure that no one was headed in my direction. This was going to be my second try, but I had a plan this time. From my first try I had learned that I needed running room. So I backed up, all the way to where the grass ended and the weeds started. Then I stood there nervously. My mouth got dry and my heart started beating faster.

I realized that this was probably the scariest thing I had ever done.

I wanted to do it, and I also didn't want to do it. But I had to show those boys and my brother that I could do it. With the weather starting to get warmer, I started to sweat also. That little inner voice was telling me that I could do it and before I knew it I had started to run, then faster and faster. I was nearing the wall when all of a sudden I panicked. I tried to slow down, but I was too close to stop, so I threw up my hands and arms to help cushion my collision with that brick wall. Amazingly, it worked, but the impact knocked the wind out of me. I stood there for a minute, regaining my breath and waiting for my heart to slow down. By now the recess bell was ringing. I composed myself and walked from around the side of the school building and calmly got in line. I was quiet for the rest of the afternoon.

Now, you would think that I had had enough of trying to run up the wall, but I hadn't. I was just getting started. For the next two weeks the boys played the running up the wall game a few times, but not as much as they had in the early spring. Most of the time they were off doing whatever it is that boys do at school. But, I hadn't forgotten what they had told me earlier in the spring. So, I kept practicing whenever there was nobody on the side of the building. I could see that I was getting better, but it was still hard and scary. I had pretty much given up the swing for that school year. I had something more important to do. I never told anyone, but during that time I got a few scrapes and scratches. I was a little sore and I had one bruise; all of this came from running up the wall or attempting to run up the wall.

The most important thing I learned was that I needed to start running from a certain distance. Once I found out what that distance was, I marked it and I started there every time. If I didn't start there, I hit the wall every time. One time I went home with a nasty looking scrape on one of my knees. When my grandmother Aint Tankie asked me what happened, I told her that I fell in the gravel driveway getting on the school bus. Another time I tore my dress at the waist and my teacher had to pin it up with a safety pin. When Aint Tankie asked me what happened, I told her that my friend was chasing me at recess. Then I added she had tried to stop me by pulling on my dress. Both times she told me to be more careful.

It was getting close to the end of the school year and I had to show the boys that I could run up the wall before school ended. It had to be the school building wall, because it was the only brick building that most of us had been inside of. We were not allowed to play near the few brick buildings we had in town. Everyone we knew including us lived in a wooden house and you can't run up those walls. A few weeks before school year ended, I was ready. I hadn't hit the wall in a while.

I went to the side wall a couple of times, but the boys weren't playing there. Then one day I went there and the boys were running up the wall. I asked them if I could run up the wall. They laughed at me, then they said no again, but I just stood there and watched them. After a while they asked what I was looking at, then told me to go play with the girls, in front of the school. Well, I folded my arms and said, "no, I want to run up the wall."

My brother walked over to me and said, "Loretta go play with the girls." I looked up at him and said, "you can't tell me what to do, I want to run up the wall." The other boys were starting to get frustrated, but I still stood there. All of us were staring at my brother, Junior. The boys had that look that said make your sister go play with the girls. My face had a definite, "no" expression on it. My poor brother was caught in the middle and his facial expression showed frustration. Finally, he said, "Loretta, go", I looked at him and said, "no."

Then his friends started telling me, "girls can't run up the wall, I don't know why you want to try it; suppose you get hurt?" That's when I blurted out, "I won't hurt myself, I been practicing!" Oh, they laughed and laughed at what I had said. The more they laughed the angrier I got and I started shouting, "I can do it! I can do it! I can do it!" As I was saying this, I started backing up to where the grass stopped and the weeds started. Out of the corner of my eye, I could see my marker. They had no idea what I was doing. Then, all of a sudden I stopped. I took in a deep breath, then

I let it out and before they knew what was happening, I started running. Those boys and my brother jumped back and cleared the way for me.

Back then, we didn't know anything about counting seconds, but we did know 1-2-3-4-5- ... All of us knew that with this game, once you start running, you only had 1-2 and maybe 3 to think about slowing down or stopping. If you decided after 2 or 3 it was too late, you were going to hit the wall and nothing could stop you. I don't know how to describe or explain what I was feeling at that moment. But between being mad and my heart racing, it seemed like I was running in slow motion. When I realized that my pace was off, it was too late for me to stop. I tried to raise my arms up for some protection against the impact, but I didn't have enough time.

I knew that I was going to hit the wall head on and I didn't have time to do anything about it. The last thing I remembered was my head and then my hands hitting the wall. When I woke up, I was on the ground. I lay there half dazed on my back. My brother and his friends were all kneeling around me. I didn't see them right away; all I saw was some of the most beautiful colored stars in the sky. Junior told me later that I said, "look at the pretty stars." Then the stars started to fade and I can remember hearing my brother call my name several times. He kept asking me if I was okay. Finally, with blood streaming down my face, my brother and his friends helped me up. By then, I had a nice big hickey about the size of half an egg, right in the middle of my forehead, The same boys who were laughing at me were now practically carrying me to my teacher.

Back then they didn't rush you to the nearest hospital or take you to the nearest doctor every time something happened. Besides that we didn't have a doctor in Wardell. The nearest doctor and hospital was in Hayti or Caruthersville. So the teacher had the boys help me to the classroom. She asked me if I was okay and how I felt. I said, "alright." The teacher took a piece of white rag from a box she had in her desk drawer and wiped away the blood. She went back into the box and got some turpentine and coal oil and mixed them together and put some on my head. Then, she put some of this mixture on another piece of white rag and tied it around my head. I was told to sit there in the room at the table until recess was over. And that was it.

When I got home that afternoon my grandmother asked me what happened, I told her the truth. I knew what she was going to tell me before she said it. She told me that I couldn't play the run up the wall game anymore. I said, "yes ma'am." After that day I was ready to give up trying to run up the wall anyway. It really was a game for boys and not for girls.

Besides that, summer was coming and I had just turned eight years old. I was a big girl and I had plans. Aint Tankie had already said that we could ride our bikes down to the river. They said that the old graveyard had haints in it. I always wanted to see a haint. Aint Tankie had told us not to to go into the graveyard, but I was a big girl now and I knew she wouldn't mind. But the best thing of all was, my cousin Doris Faye was coming for a long visit. And then, there was this big old – well that's another story for another day.

Our Christmas Eve Job

The first four Christmases that I can remember were spent in the Missouri Bootheel. Starting about a week before Christmas Eve the smell of cakes and pies filled our small country house. My grandmother Aint Tankie had started teaching me how to cook, so she let me help her make all of the cakes and pies. Although I enjoyed helping her make those wonderful sweet treats, it was torture not being able to eat any of them before Christmas Eve. My cooking lessons did not include our Christmas Eve meal. Aint Tankie always liked to cook those dishes herself. So a few days before Christmas, my grandmother would start preparing the tasty dishes that made up our Christmas Eve supper.

For as long as I could remember, my brother Junior, my cousin and I had been responsible for putting up the Christmas decorations. Our task filled us with excitement, even though we didn't have a lot to decorate. We had a few things that Aint Tankie had saved from year to year. But we made the majority of our Christmas decoration each year. As kids, the homemade decorations were always fun to make. Our only worry was whether we had enough for the tree. We never knew beforehand what the tree was going to look like. Like most kids, we had dreams of this "big" tree, but every year our tree was small and sparse. It didn't really bother us that our tree was small, but every year we still wished for a "big tree." We always loved our tree and thought it was beautiful and we always gingerly decorated it. Then we would painstakingly place the remaining pieces of decoration throughout the house.

One particular Christmas Eve, we could barely contain ourselves. All of the delicious smells mingled together and filled every room in the house. Christmas Eve was the only holiday of the year that everyone got all dressed up. Everyone would put on their Sunday best for supper that night. Everyone always looked so nice and this added to my excitement. Just before dusk our Christmas Eve celebration would officially start. Mr. Fred and several of our neighbors always joined us for supper, and guess what they usually brought—more cakes.

My brother, cousin and I always knew when it was near supper time. When my grandmother would start uncovering all of the cakes and pies, we knew that it was almost time to eat. Then she would uncover the rest of the food on the table. The meats and biscuits were always the last things she would put on the table. She always put the smoked ham and baked turkey in the center of the table and the biscuits went on the corner near the cakes and pies. At this point we knew that it wouldn't be long before she would have all of us gather around the table for the blessing. We also knew that Aint Tankie was probably going to ask Mr. Fred to bless the food.

And she did. My grandmother asked Mr. Fred to bless our supper. Oh, he prayed for the longest time! Mr. Fred stood at the end of the table where all of the cakes and pies were. Then he asked all of the kids, or "God's children" as he called us, to come and stand next to him. During his long prayer we had to stand there and look at all of those good smelling sweet treats. It was torture standing so close to all of those cakes and pies while Mr. Fred prayed that long prayer. All we could do was look at each other and wonder if he was ever going to finish praying. We couldn't move and we definitely couldn't raise our arms high enough to get a finger lick of icing.

We hoped that would be the last time that Mr. Fred would be blessing our Christmas Eve supper. Mr. Fred had always stopped by every now and then to check on us and see if my grandmother had anything that needed to be done. But after the last Christmas he had started coming around more often. He was around during the winter months, in the spring, the summer, the fall and now again on Christmas Eve. Throughout the year when he stopped by around supper time, my grandmother always asked him to stay for supper. He always accepted and she always asked him to bless the food. I can't remember hearing Mr. Fred ever saying a short prayer. Now, I liked Mr. Fred, because he always gave me the nicest compliments when I fixed him some of my sweet flapjacks. But he just prayed too long.

Deep down inside, I knew that my grandmother was going to ask Mr. Fred to bless our Christmas Eve supper again. With his sweet tooth, I knew that he was going to stand by the cakes and pies to pray. And I knew that he was going to ask God's children to stand beside him again. I couldn't handle another one of his long prayers while standing in front of all of those cakes and pies. I didn't want to go through that torture again. So I went to my brother and cousin and reminded them of our last Christmas Eve. Then I asked them if they could resist being that close to all of those desserts again this year. They said no!

I told Junior and my cousin about a plan I had come up with. A plan where we could have all the icing we wanted before Mr. Fred blessed the food. I called my plan the icing trick, but my brother called it, our Christmas Eve Job. I guess you could say that Mr. Fred was the reason the three of us needed a Christmas Eve Job. I had learned the icing trick from my grandmother. Part of my cooking lessons was to watch her when she cooked and also when I helped her cook. While we were baking the Christmas Eve cakes she showed me how to make the cakes look pretty and neat. She would run one finger around the area where the cake met the cake plate and remove some of the icing. She always put the extra icing back into the bowl. She never once licked her fingers. How could she resist butter cream and chocolate icing? How could she resist it?

The first part of our job was easy. The plan was, one by one we had to make our way out of the living room unnoticed. Then, once we were in the dining room, we would secretively sneak a finger of icing from every cake on the table. I told them that if we weren't careful, Aint Tankie would surely notice the difference. I gave them some more instructions on how to make their licks unnoticeable, and we were ready. If our plan was successful, then Mr. Fred could stand over the cakes and pies, with God's children, and pray. He could pray for as long as he wanted to because we would be okay. Mr. Fred said that he had a sweet tooth, but each of us had a mouth full of sweet teeth and we wanted all of our sweet teeth to be satisfied.

When Aint Tankie finished putting all of the food on the table, she came into the living room and joined the conversation for a few minutes. The time was right and we went into action. While everyone was laughing and talking, each of us would slowly get up from our strategic locations. One by one from prearranged directions we approached the dining room doorway. I slowly looked back, then I gave Junior an okay tap on the shoulder. We nonchalantly entered the dining room. Then we quickly disappeared up against the wall that divided the living room from the dining room. This was also the wall that was the closest to the cakes.

We stood there for a few seconds quietly laughing. We salivated as we thought about all of the sweet treats that awaited us then we headed for the cakes. From this point on, each of us was free to start wherever we wanted. We didn't worry about making a mistake, because we knew our jobs well. There were chocolate cakes, a coconut cake, butter cream cakes, a jelly cake, caramel cakes, some kind of cake with a glaze, and a few cakes I didn't recognize, but all of them had icing on them. I reminded them one last time to be very careful with our icing lines. There was an art to what we were doing. We ran one finger along the edge of each cake where the cake met the plate. We knew not to dig too deep into the icing and we knew how long to make our line so that no one noticed.

Once our job was complete we licked our fingers and lips until they were clean. We didn't have a mirror, so we checked each other's faces to make sure we had gotten rid of all of the evidence. Then we returned to the wall. We stood there for a few seconds, regaining our composure. Then one by one we quietly reentered the living room. Each of us returned to our strategic locations and nonchalantly sat down. We glanced across the room at each other with smiles of contentment on our faces. Our Christmas Eve Job was completed until the next year.

Soon after our return Aint Tankie asked Mr. Fred to bless the food. Sure enough he did exactly what we thought he would do. With all of God's children standing by his side, Mr. Fred prayed another long Christmas Eve prayer. But that year we were fine and all of those cakes and pies didn't tempt God's children. We just stood there with smiles on our faces and when he finished, we ate supper. The three of us did our Christmas Eve Jobs for the next two years. In 1955 we returned to St. Louis. Christmas Eve was very different in the city and we never had another Christmas Eve Job.

To this day when I cut into a layer cake and see the excess icing around the edge, sometimes I have to sneak a finger lick. When I do this it brings back memories of the three of us and our "Christmas Eve Job." We thought we were smart, but I often wondered, "did we really get away with it, like we thought we did?" I never asked my grandmother if she knew what we were doing on those Christmas Eves right before the food was blessed.

Maybe I really didn't want to know whether my grandmother knew. But I did notice one thing; my grandmother never asked Mr. Fred to bless the Christmas Eve supper until we returned to the living room and sat down. Amazingly, we always seem to make it back without being noticed and just seconds before she would interrupt all of the laughing and talking and say, "Fred, would you bless the food?"

A Roman Candle Christmas

My childhood Christmases in the Missouri Bootheel were very different from the ones I later experienced when I returned to St. Louis to live. In Wardell, I can remember waking up on Christmas Eve morning, wanting the sun to go down so that we could have supper and start waiting for midnight. Every Christmas Eve we got to stay up past midnight because of the fireworks. Christmas Eve was also the only time we were allowed to eat all of the desserts we wanted. All of us were excited between the sweet desserts, the fireworks and Santa Claus coming. It always worried me, whether I had been naughty or nice, and whether I was going to get the gift I wanted. We already knew that we had to go to bed and go to sleep right after the fireworks. My grandmother always told us that Santa Claus wouldn't come if we were awake.

Didn't she realize? With so much going on in our house on Christmas Eve, who could sleep? I didn't want to miss any of it. Every year I always worried and thought, "what if I can't go to sleep, will Santa still come?"

On Christmas Eve after supper, everyone had dessert. We would sit around and eat sweet treats while laughing and talking about any and everything. Then somebody would always tell a story about one of our past Christmases. That would remind someone else about another Christmas, then someone else would remember another story. Eventually someone would start telling a story that wasn't about Christmas. But, somehow we always ended with someone telling another Christmas story. Somewhere during our evening of laughter and storytelling Mr. Fred or his brother Mr. Sampson or Aint Tankie would bring up one of their Christmas Give Stories.

I always liked to hear their Christmas Give Stories. Christmas Give was a game that the adults used to play on each other on Christmas day.

The rules never changed, but the way they surprised each other on Christmas day changed each year. The tricky part was that you never knew what time one of them was going to pop up. The game was about who could get to the other person's house without being seen and be the first to say Christmas Give! But if the other person saw you coming and said "Christmas Give" first, they won. Usually they did this very early in the morning, but sometimes they would change the time. Then they would laugh and talk about who surprised who. The loser always talked about how they were going to get them next Christmas.

Sometimes we would help Aint Tankie watch for the others, so that she could yell Christmas Give before they saw her. Whenever we saw one of them first, we would run to Aint Tankie all excited. We would be screaming, "somebody's coming, somebody's coming!" We never helped her watch very long, because it was Christmas day and we were excited, we wanted to go and play. But the adults really seemed to enjoy this game. I think surprising each other was fun for them, but I liked getting gifts and treats; that was fun to me.

When I used to think back about the Christmas Give Game, it made me a little sad. I could never remember my grandmother or any adult getting a real Christmas gift. I used to wish– if I'd had some money back then, I would have bought all of them gifts. But back then everyone barely earned enough to live on; nobody had extra money. The adults usually had very little or no money to spend on themselves. Sadly, that was a way of life for the majority of field laborers. Being much older today, I realize that the Christmas Give Game was not about material things. It was about friends and friendships.

As kids we enjoyed dessert time, the stories and more desserts, but our minds were always on the fireworks. We would sit there wiggling in our seats while listening to the stories and waiting for midnight. I can remember asking my grandmother what time it was, all through the evening. Her answer was always not yet, but, I knew that one of those times she was going to say, it's time. The closer we got to midnight the more I felt like I was going to burst. The giggles set in and I couldn't sit still. Then finally, I asked is it time? and she said "yes."

Everybody put on their coats and bundled up. Even though it was always very cold around Christmas, we never wore gloves. We needed our hands free to handle the fireworks. The three of us hurried outside first. We were ready for the fireworks to start. Except for our Christmas Eve Job, this was always the most exciting time of the holiday season. Immediately, my brother and cousin found themselves a spot and started shooting their firecrackers and other fireworks. Some of the men were always near my brother and cousin, in case they needed them.

I always stood beside my grandmother and waited patiently for her to light my first roman candle and hand it to me. Standing there, on the outside I looked calm, but inside I would be shaking, not from the cold, but from the excitement. I could hear Junior and my cousin shooting their fireworks while laughing and talking. It seemed like it was taking Aint Tankie forever to light one of my roman candles. Finally one of them was ready and she handed it to me. I think my grandmother could see that I was excited and nervous, because she asked me if I was all right. I looked up at her and nodded my head. I was always nervous when it was time to shoot my first roman candle. But, now all I wanted to do was get started

As I stood there with my arm extended over my head, swirling my roman candle around and around, I could hear it making that bubbling sound. The sound was letting me know that it was getting ready. As kids we used to call the bubbling sound cooking. Oh, the cooking sound was building and getting louder and louder. (To this day I have not figured out how as kids we knew when to stop swirling the roman candle and shoot it.) When the cooking sound got to a certain point I would stop swirling the roman candle. Then I would point it straight up towards the dark night sky, filled with stars. I always stood very still while looking up, my heart pounding. And then it happened. The cooking stopped for a second, then this big ball shot out. The ball would fly high into the night sky and then all of a sudden: puwww! The ball would burst above our heads, creating a beautiful blanket of multicolored stars that blended in with the white stars of the dark night sky.

I watched as the blanket of colorful stars quickly faded away. Then I would swirl my roman candle again. I could hear it making that bubbling sound again. The sound would get louder and louder and then I would stop swirling it. I would stand there very still, anticipating what was about to happen. I would point my roman candle straight up again as far as I could reach. The cooking sound stopped for a second and then another big ball would shoot out. It would fly high into the night sky and then all of a sudden it would happen again (puwww!). The ball would burst above our heads, creating another beautiful blanket of multicolor stars. They too blended in with the white stars of the night sky. I repeated these steps again and again until my roman candle stopped bubbling and was silent.

Excited, I would look up at Aint Tankie and try to wait patiently for her to hand me another roman candle. Then the whole process started all over again. I stood there the whole time, frozen in my tracks with excitement each time the ball shot out and went puwww! I was excited and peaceful at the same time. This was a feeling that my childlike mind couldn't absorb, but it was a good feeling. Even though each blanket of colored stars always faded away quickly, no child could feel safer than I did at that moment. Looking up and seeing that twinkling protective blanket covering us and being surrounded by everyone I loved, as a child, I felt completely safe.

When the last ball shot out of my roman candle and went high into the night sky and burst, the bubbling sound stopped. I stood there and watched one last blanket of stars form above our heads, then quickly fade away. I continued to stand there for a while. As my eyes readjusted to the night sky, I could see the blanket of white stars that covered us every night. My trance-like state slowly started to fade. Once again I could hear my brother's and cousin's fireworks. In the distance, I could hear our neighbor's fireworks and see their roman candles. Soon after that, one by one, all of the firework celebrations ended. The fireworks lasted for about fifteen minutes, but to me, it seemed much shorter.

As we started talking about the fireworks, in the distance, we heard a few more firecrackers. Then, we heard puwww and everyone stopped talking. Our neighbor was shooting their last roman candle. When we heard it we stood there and watched. We watched until the last burst from the roman candle went puwww in the night sky. All of us knew that our Christmas Eve Celebration was over until next year.

I was seven years old my first Christmas in Wardell, and four years later we returned to St. Louis. Sadly, they didn't shoot fireworks on Christmas Eve in the city. In the late 1950's my grandmother came to live with us. One day we were talking and I asked her why Wardell had fireworks on Christmas Eve and St. Louis didn't. That's when Aint Tankie told me, "the fireworks and your roman candles—that was our way of celebrating Jesus' birthday." When she told me this, I think I finally understood that feeling that I couldn't explain. For the first time it made sense to me. What I was feeling back then was God's love and protection.

I would love to have just one more roman candle Christmas Eve. But if I don't, I know that long, long ago on a cold clear night the North Star could be seen for miles. The Heavenly Host could be heard singing Glory to God in the Highest. And, then there were the three wise men that brought gifts to a little stable where the baby Jesus lay sleeping in a manger.

When I remember our Christmas Eves, I know that every year on a cold clear night in the Missouri Bootheel we also made a joyful noise that could be heard for miles. Our gift was small, but it too could be seen for miles. With the little we had we celebrated the birth of Jesus, in the grandest way we could, with fireworks and roman candles, and I was a part of it. Now I know our gift was acceptable, even though it may have faded quickly. The multicolored stars from my roman candle mixed with the stars in the night sky and formed a heavenly blanket. And, that memory will remain in my heart, forever.

We were poor, but on that night, with our fireworks, we shared what we had in the grandest way we knew how to. And, for a few seconds we were covered with a beautiful blanket of multicolor stars that mixed with the night stars. We were blessed to see God's love. The stars from my roman candles may have faded in a few seconds, but the night stars, are with us always. I believe that was God's way of letting us know that our Gift was acceptable. We were not poor in his eyesight. We were richer than our biggest dream, because God had given us the gift of love. "The gift of love for each other."

About the Author

Loretta Washington, Master Storyteller, Writer, and Multipurpose Workshop Presenter.

For years I have written and spoken the words, "I'm on a journey and I hope I never arrive." My storytelling journey has been going on for more than twenty-two years and I'm still enjoying it. To be blessed and respected in an art form such as storytelling is indeed an honor. You can ask anyone I know and they will tell you that I don't take what I do lightly. I have been giving the gift of sharing the spoken word and I share it from my heart.

I wrote my first two personal stories in 2000. I started telling those and other personal stories in 2002. Since then I haven't stopped writing and sharing a variety of personal and family stories. We all have personal and family stories, ranging from when you were a child until now, and they will continue to grow. The stories are endless; I haven't stopped living and writing them.

I was born in St. Louis, Missouri, and I've lived most of my life here, except for the six years I spent in the Missouri Bootheel, in the little town of Wardell. In 1949 my mother and father separated and later divorced. My mother took my brother, Junior, and me to live in Wardell with my grandmother (Aint Tankie) and my great grandmother (Ellen).

I left St. Louis at age four and returned at age ten. I often refer to my six years in the bootheel as my formative years. Some of my fondest and most heartfelt memories of life originated from the time I spent in that little country town with my grandmother and my great grandmother.

Aint Tankie was very dear to me and her noteworthy role in this book is very deserving. I proudly honor Aint Tankie and my great grandmother for the love they showed me. I will never forget the roles each one of them played in laying a strong foundation for me. I have never had another disciplinarian in my life who was loved so much by me and so many, as Aint Tankie was. To this day, I still wonder sometimes how she always seemed to have all of the right answers, all the time.

In writing these stories, many memories from my childhood continued to surface. After more than twenty-two years as a traditional, spoken word artist, I still have some stories that are screaming to be written and told. I believe that my love for this generational art form came from my great grandmother. I have enjoyed sharing the stories in *My Corner Of The Porch* with you. I hope you enjoy reading them time and time again for years. "What a fantastic journey I'm on. I get to share the written and spoken word with everyone I encounter. I hope I never arrive."

Loretta Washington, 2016
St. Louis, Missouri.
E-Mail: bjsadmc@hotmail.com
Website: *http://lorettawstoryteller.wix.com/storyteller*

Photographs

Aint Tankie, age 90

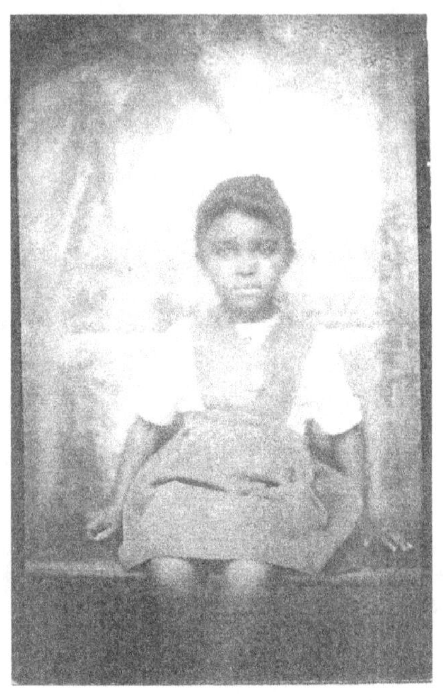

Doris Faye, age 4

Loretta, age 7

Junior, age 12

Loretta Washington at Wardell, 2003

Old cotton gin, Wardell

The road Loretta Washington walked to catch the school bus, Wardell

Water Tower, Wardell